This book is a gift
From
Mom + Dad

Also by Tove Jansson

Finn Family Moomintroll
Comet in Moominland

Moominsummer
Madness

Moominsummer Madness

Tove Jansson

TRANSLATED BY
THOMAS WARBURTON

A SUNBURST BOOK
FARRAR · STRAUS · GIROUX

CONTENTMENTS

Moominsummer Madness

CHAPTER I

About a bark boat and a volcano

Moominmamma was sitting on the front steps in the sun, rigging a model bark schooner.

"One big sail on the mainmast, and one on the foremast, and several small three-cornered ones to the bowsprit, if I remember rightly," she thought.

The rudder was a ticklish job, and the hold an odder one. Moominmamma had cut a tiny bark hatch, and when she laid it on, it fitted snugly and neatly over the hold.

"Just in case of a hurricane," she said to herself with a happy sigh.

By her side on the steps, knees under chin, sat the Mymble's daughter, looking on. She saw Moominmamma next tack the stays with small glass-headed pins, each of a different colour. The mast-heads were already flying bright red pennants.

"For whom is it?" asked the Mymble's daughter respectfully.

"For Moomintroll," replied his mamma, and searched her work-basket for something for an anchor cable.

"Don't push me about!" cried a small voice from the basket.

"Dear me," said Moominmamma, "here's your little sister in my work-basket again! She's going to hurt herself on the pins and needles one day."

"My!" said the Mymble's daughter menacingly and tried to pull her sister out of a skein of wool. "Come out at once!"

But Little My managed to crawl deeper into the wool, where she disappeared completely.

"Such a nuisance she turned out so very small," complained the Mymble's daughter. "I never know where to look for her. Couldn't you make a bark boat for her, too? She could sail in the water barrel, and I'd always know where she is."

Moominmamma laughed and looked in her handbag for another piece of bark.

"Do you think this would hold Little My?" she asked.

"Certainly," said the Mymble's daughter. "But you'll have to make a small life-belt as well."

"May I cut up your knitting ball?" shouted Little My from the sewing-basket.

"By all means," replied Moominmamma. She was admiring her schooner and wondered if she had forgotten anything. As she sat holding it in her paw a big black flake of soot came floating down and landed amidships on the deck.

"Ugh," said Moominmamma and blew it away. Immediately another flake landed on her nose. Suddenly the air was full of soot.

Moominmamma rose with a sigh.

"So very annoying, this volcano," she remarked.

"Volcano?" asked Little My, and thrust an interested head out of the wool.

"Yes, it's a mountain not so very far from here, and all of a sudden it's begun spitting fire and smoke over the whole valley," explained Moominmamma. "And soot. It's always kept quiet and good ever since I married. And now, after all these years, exactly when I've finished my washing, it has to sneeze once again and blacken all the things I hung out."

"Everybody's burning up!" shouted Little My happily. "And everybody's houses and gardens and playthings and little sisters and their playthings!"

"Fiddlesticks," said Moominmamma genially and whisked away another speck of soot from her nose. Then she went off to look for Moomintroll.

★   ★   ★

Under the slope, a little to the right of Moominpappa's hammock tree, was a large pond of clear, brown water. The Mymble's daughter always insisted that it had no bottom in the middle. Perhaps she was right. Around the edges broad and shining leaves grew for dragonflies and skimming-beetles to rest on, and below the surface spidery creatures used to row wrigglingly along, trying to look important. Further down, the pond-frog's eyes glinted like gold, and sometimes you could catch a quick glimpse of her mysterious relatives that lived deep down in the mud.

Moomintroll was lying in his customary place (or one of his places), curled up on the green-and-yellow moss with his tail carefully tucked in under him.

He looked gravely and contentedly down into the water while he listened to the rustle of wings and the drowsy buzz of bees around him.

"It's for me," he thought. "I'm sure it's for me. She always makes the first bark boat of the summer for the one she likes most. Then she muddles it all away a little, because she doesn't want anybody to feel hurt. If that water-spider goes crawling eastwards, there'll be no dinghy. If it goes westwards,

she's made a dinghy so small that you hardly dare take it in your paw."

The spider crawled off eastwards, and tears welled up in Moomintroll's eyes.

At that moment there was a rustling in the grass, and his mother thrust out her head between the tufts.

"Hello," she said. "I've got something for you."

She bent down and floated the schooner with great care. It balanced beautifully over its own reflection and started away on the port tack as if manned by old salts.

Moomintroll saw at a glance that she had forgotten the dinghy.

He rubbed his nose friendlily against hers (it feels like stroking your face against white velvet) and said: "It's the nicest you've ever made."

They sat side by side in the moss and watched the schooner sail across the pond and land at the other shore beside a large leaf.

Over at the house the Mymble's daughter was shouting for her little sister. "My! My!" she yelled. "Horrible little menace! My-y-y! Come home at once so I can pull your hair!"

"She's hid somewhere again," said Moomintroll. "Remember that time we found her in your bag?"

Moominmamma nodded. She was dipping her nose in the water and looking at the bottom.

"There's a nice gleam down there," she said.

"It's your golden bracelet," said Moomintroll. "And the Snork Maiden's necklace. Good idea, isn't it?"

"Splendid," said his mother. "We'll always keep our bangles in brown pond water in the future. They're so much more beautiful that way."

★   ★   ★

On the front steps of Moominhouse stood the Mymble's daughter, nearly breaking her voice with

yelling. Little My sat quietly in one of her number-less hide-outs, just as her sister knew.

"She'd use some kind of bait instead, if she were wise," thought Little My. "Honey, for instance. And then beat me up when I came."

"Mymble," said Moominpappa from his rocking-chair. "If you keep shouting like that she'll never come."

"It's for my conscience' sake," explained the Mymble's daughter a little conceitedly. "It hurts me more than her. When Mother went away she said to me: 'Now I'm leaving your little sister in your care, and if you can't bring her up nobody can, because I've given up.'"

"I see," said Moominpappa. "Then please yell all you want to, if it takes a weight off your mind." He reached out for a piece of cake from the luncheon table, looked around him carefully, and dipped it in the cream jug.

The verandah table was laid for five. The sixth plate was under it, because the Mymble's daughter declared that she felt more independent there.

My's plate, of course, was very small, and it was placed in the shadow of the flower vase in the middle of the table.

Now Moominmamma came galloping up the garden path.

"There's no hurry, dear," said Moominpappa. "We had a snack in the pantry."

Moominmamma stopped to look at the luncheon table. The cloth was speckled over with soot.

"Oh, dear me," she said. "What a terribly hot and sooty day. Volcanoes are such a nuisance."

"If it only weren't quite so far away," said Moominpappa. "Then one could find a paperweight of real lava," he added longingly.

It really was a hot day.

Moomintroll had remained lying in his place by the pond, looking up at the sky, which had turned sparkling white like a sheet of silver. He could hear the sea-gulls squawking to each other down by the seashore.

"There's a thunderstorm coming," Moomintroll thought sleepily and rose to his feet from the moss. And as always when there was a change in the weather, dusk, or a strange light in the sky, he noticed that he was longing for Snufkin.

Snufkin was his best friend. Of course, he also liked the Snork Maiden a lot, but still it can never be quite the same with a girl.

Snufkin was a calm person who knew an immense lot of things but never talked about them unnecessarily. Only now and again he told a little about his travels, and that made one rather proud, as if Snufkin had made one a member of a secret society. Moomintroll started his winter sleep with the others when the first snow fell. But Snufkin always wandered off to the South and returned to Moominvalley in the springtime.

This spring he hadn't come back!

Moomintroll had begun waiting for him as soon as he awoke, even if he didn't tell the others. When the birds began to wing their way high over the valley, and even the snow on the northern slopes had melted, he became impatient. Never before had Snufkin been so late. And then summer came, and long grass grew all over Snufkin's camping place by the river, as if no one had ever lived there.

Moomintroll waited still, but not so eagerly any more, just reproachfully and a little tiredly.

The Snork Maiden had brought up the topic once at the dinner-table.

"How late Snufkin is this year," she said.

"Who knows, perhaps he won't come at all," said the Mymble's daughter.

"I'm sure the Groke's got him!" cried Little My. "Or he's fallen down a hole and gone to pieces!"

"Hush, dear," said Moominmamma hastily. "You know that Snufkin always comes out on top."

"But still," Moomintroll reflected on his quiet walk along the river. "There ARE Grokes and policemen. And abysses to fall in. And it happens that people freeze to death, and blow up in the air, and fall in the sea, and catch herring-bones in their throats, and a lot of other things.

"The big world is dangerous. Where there's no one to know one and no one to know what one likes and what one's afraid of. And that's where Snufkin's walking along now in his old green hat . . . And there's the Park Keeper who is his great enemy. A terrible, terrible enemy . . ."

Moomintroll stopped on the bridge and stared bleakly down at the water. At that moment a paw touched him lightly on the shoulder. Moomintroll turned with quite a jump.

"Oh, it's you," he said.

"I don't know what to do," said the Snork Maiden, giving him an imploring look under her fringe.

She wore a wreath of violets around her ears and had felt bored since morning.

Moomintroll made a friendly and slightly preoccupied sound.

"Let's play," said the Snork Maiden. "Let's play that I'm a wondrous beauty who gets kidnapped by you."

"I really don't know if I'm in the mood for it," replied Moomintroll.

The Snork Maiden drooped her ears, and he hastily brushed his nose against hers and said: "There's no need to imagine that you're a wondrous beauty, because that's what you are. Perhaps I'll feel like kidnapping you tomorrow instead."

*　　　*　　　*

The June day passed, and dusk was falling, but the weather remained just as warm.

The air was almost scorchingly dry and full of swirling soot, and the whole Moomin family drooped and became dull and silent and unsociable. Finally Moominmamma had an idea and resolved that everybody was to sleep out in the garden that night. She made up their beds in nice places, and by every bed she placed a little lamp so that nobody would feel lonely.

Moomintroll and the Snork Maiden curled up beneath the jasmines. But they couldn't sleep.

It was no ordinary night. It was silent in an uncanny way.

"It's so warm," complained the Snork Maiden. "I keep tossing and turning, and the sheet's horrible, and soon I'll have to start thinking about unpleasant things!"

"Same here," said Moomintroll.

He sat up and looked around him in the garden. The others seemed to be asleep, and the lamps were burning quietly by the beds.

Suddenly the jasmine bushes stirred and shivered violently.

"Did you see that?" said the Snork Maiden.

"Now they're quiet again," replied Moomintroll.

As he said it their lamp turned over in the grass.

The flowers on the ground gave a start, and then a narrow crack came slowly creeping across the lawn. It crept and crept and finally disappeared under the mattress. Then it widened. Earth and sand began to trickle down in it, and a moment later Moomintroll's toothbrush slipped straight down into the dark and yawning earth.

"It was a brand-new one!" exclaimed Moomintroll. "Can you see it?"

He applied his nose to the crack and peered down.

Suddenly the earth closed again, with a light whupping sound.

"Brand-new," repeated Moomintroll blankly. "Blue."

"Just fancy if your tail had been caught!" the

Snork Maiden consoled him. "Then you'd have had to sit here for the rest of your life!"

Moomintroll rose speedily. "Come along," he said. "We'll sleep on the verandah."

Moominpappa was already standing by the steps and sniffing the air. There was an anxious rustling in the garden, flocks of birds were flying up, small feet hurrying through the grass.

Little My thrust out her head from the sunflower by the steps and shouted happily: "Here goes!"

A faint rumbling sounded from deep under their feet, and from the kitchen came a loud crash as the pots and pans dropped off the shelves.

"Breakfast?" cried Moominmamma, startled out of her sleep. "What's up?"

"Nothing, dear," answered Moominpappa. "I suppose it's only the volcano again . . . Just think of all those paperweights . . ."

Now the Mymble's daughter was awake also. Everybody gathered at the verandah railing, wide-eyed and sniffing.

"Where's that volcano?" asked Moomintroll.

"On a little island off the coast," replied his father. "A black little island where nothing grows."

"Don't you think it's just a teeny bit dangerous?" whispered Moomintroll and put his paw in Moominpappa's.

"Oh, yes," replied Moominpappa kindly. "A weeny bit."

Moomintroll nodded happily.

It was at that moment they heard the great rumble.

It came rolling up from across the sea, first low and mumbling, then growing stronger and stronger.

In the fair night they could see something enormous rise high over the tree-tops of the forest, like a great wall that grew and grew with a white and foaming crest.

"I suppose we'd better go into the drawing-room now," said Moominmamma.

They had no more than got their tails inside the door when the flood wave came crashing through Moominvalley and drenched everything in dark-

ness. The house rocked slightly but didn't lose its foothold. It was soundly built and a very good house. But after a while the drawing-room furniture began to float around. The family then moved upstairs and sat down to wait for the storm to blow over.

"I haven't seen such weather since my young days," said Moominpappa brightly and lit a candle.

Outside, the night was in full uproar, cracking and banging things about and thumping heavy waves against the shutters.

Moominmamma absentmindedly seated herself in the rocking-chair and set it slowly rocking.

"Is this the end of the world?" Little My asked curiously.

"That's the very least," replied the Mymble's daughter. "Try to be good now if you can find the time, because in a little while we're all going to heaven."

"Heaven?" asked Little My. "Do we have to? And how does one get back again?"

Something heavy crashed against the house, and the candle flickered.

"Mamma," Moomintroll whispered.

"Yes, dear," said Moominmamma.

"I forgot the bark boat by the pool."

"It'll be there tomorrow," replied Moominmamma. Suddenly she stopped rocking and exclaimed: "Dear me, how could I!"

"What?" said the Snork Maiden with a start.

"The dinghy," said Moominmamma. "I've forgotten to make a dinghy. I had a definite feeling that I'd forgotten something important."

"Now it's reached the damper," announced Moominpappa. He kept on running down to the drawing-room to measure the water-level. They looked towards the stairs and thought of all the things that would have been nicer dry.

"Did anybody take the hammock in?" asked Moominpappa suddenly.

No one had remembered the hammock.

"Good," said Moominpappa. "It was a horrid colour."

The swish and hiss of the water outside made them sleepy, and one after another they curled up on the floor and went to sleep. But before he blew the candle out Moominpappa set the alarm-clock at seven.

He was terribly curious about what had happened outside.

CHAPTER II

About diving for breakfast

At last daylight came back again.

It began as a narrow strip that wriggled along the horizon before daring to climb higher in the sky.

The weather was calm, and pleasant. But the waves, in excited confusion, were washing new shores that had never before met the sea. The volcano that had started all the fuss had calmed down. It sighed wearily now and then, and breathed a little ash towards the sky.

At seven sharp the alarm-clock shrilled.

The Moomin family awoke at once, and everybody hurried to the window to take a look. They lifted Little My up on the sill, and the Mymble's daughter took a firm hold of her dress to keep her from falling.

The world was changed indeed.

Only a piece of the wood-shed roof remained over the swirling water. A few people, probably from the forest, sat huddled on it, shuddering with cold.

All the trees grew straight out of water, and the mountain ridges around Moominvalley were now clusters of rocky islands.

"I liked it better the old way," said Moominmamma. She screwed up her eyes against the morning sun that came rolling out of the whole chaos, red and big like an autumn moon.

"And no morning coffee," said Moominpappa.

Moominmamma glanced towards the stairs that disappeared into troubled waters. She thought of her kitchen. Her thoughts moved on to the coffee tin on the chimney-piece and she wondered if she had remembered to screw the lid on. She sighed.

"I'll dive for it," suggested Moomintroll, whose thoughts had moved exactly the same way.

"You couldn't hold your breath for so long, dear," replied Mamma anxiously.

Moominpappa gave them a strange look. "I've often thought," he said musingly, "that one ought to look at one's abode sometimes from the ceiling instead of from the floor."

"Do you mean . . . ?" said Moomintroll delightedly.

Moominpappa nodded. He disappeared into his room and presently returned with an auger and a narrow saw.

Everybody gathered around him and watched interestedly while he worked. Moominpappa found sawing his own floor to pieces just a little dreadful, but at the same time highly satisfying.

★   ★   ★

A few minutes later Moominmamma for the first time saw her kitchen from the ceiling. Enchanted, she looked down to a dimly lit, light-green aquarium. She could glimpse the stove, sink, and sloppail down on the bottom. But all the chairs and the table were floating around near the ceiling.

"Dear me, how funny," said Moominmamma and burst out laughing.

She laughed so hard that she had to take to the rocking-chair again. It felt very refreshing to see one's kitchen like that.

"A good thing I emptied the slops," she said and dried her eyes. "And forgot to bring in fire-wood!"

"I'll dive now, Mamma," said Moomintroll.

"Tell him not to, please, please," said the Snork Maiden anxiously.

"Well, why should I?" replied his mother. "If he thinks it's thrilling."

Moomintroll stood quite still for a moment and took a few calm breaths. Then he plunged down into the kitchen.

He swam straight to the pantry and managed to open the door. Inside, the water was white with milk, with a few specks of loganberry jam thrown in. A couple of loaves of bread passed him slowly, followed by a school of macaroni. Moomintroll snatched the butter dish, caught one of the wheaten loaves, and swerved back by the chimney-piece for Moominmamma's coffee tin. Then he rose to the ceiling and took a long breath.

"There, I *had* screwed the lid on!" said his mother delightedly. "This is quite a picnic. Do you think you can find the coffee pot and some cups, too?"

They had never had a more exciting breakfast.

They picked a chair that no one had ever liked and chopped it up. Unfortunately, the sugar had

melted, but Moomintroll found a tin of treacle instead. His father spooned marmalade straight from the pot, and Little My busied herself with the auger, boring her way through the loaf without anybody saying a word.

Time and again Moomintroll dived for new things, and then he splashed water around the whole room.

"I'm not washing any dishes today," Moomin-mamma said hilariously. "Who knows, perhaps I'll never wash dishes any more. But please, can't we try to save the drawing-room suite before it spoils?"

★   ★   ★

Outside, the sun had warmed, and the heavy sea had subsided.

The people on the wood-shed roof chirped up and began to feel provoked at the disorder around them.

"In my mother's time these things never hap-pened," exclaimed a disgusted mousewife, combing her tail with great vehemence. "They simply weren't allowed! But the times are changing and young people do what they please nowadays."

A serious little beast eagerly moved closer to the others and said: "I don't think any young people could have made the great flood wave. We're too small in this valley to make waves in anything other than pools or pails. Or teacups."

"Is the young man poking fun at somebody?" asked the mousewife, raising her eyebrows.

"Certainly not," replied the serious little beast. "But I've pondered and pondered all the night. Where do such waves come from when there's been no gale? It's very interesting, don't you see, and I think that either—"

"And what's the young man's name, may I ask?" the mousewife interrupted him.

"Whomper," replied the small beast without vexation. "If we could only *understand* how it all came about, then the big wave would appear perfectly natural."

"Natural, indeed!" squeaked a fat little Misabel at his side. "Whomper doesn't understand! Everything's gone wrong for me, simply everything! The day before yesterday someone had put a cone in my shoe to taunt me with my big feet, and yesterday a Hemulen laughed very meaningly as he passed my window. And then this!"

"Did the big flood come just to vex Misabel?" asked a little Squeak, impressed.

"I've never said that," answered Misabel, on the verge of tears. "Whoever would think of me or do anything for my sake? Least of all a flood wave."

"Perhaps the cone had simply fallen down from a pine?" suggested Whomper helpfully. "If it was a pine cone. Otherwise it must have been a spruce cone. If your shoe would be big enough to hold a spruce cone?"

"I know my feet are large," Misabel mumbled bitterly.

"I'm only trying to explain," said Whomper.

"This is a matter of feeling," said Misabel. "And such things can *never* be explained."

"I suppose not," said Whomper dejectedly.

The mousewife meanwhile had finished doing up her tail and now aimed her interest at the Moominhouse.

"They're rescuing their furniture," she said, craning her neck. (I see the sofa's rather threadbare.) "And they've had breakfast! Great goodness, some people do know how to keep their heads above water. The Snork Maiden is doing her hair." (While we drown.) "Indeed. Now they're lifting the sofa out on the roof to dry. Now they're hoisting the

flag. By the tail of my tail, some people are very free and easy."

Moominmamma leant over the balcony rail and shouted a greeting.

"Good morning!" Whomper cried back eagerly. "May we pay you a visit? Or is it too early? Shall we come in the afternoon instead?"

"Please come," said Moominmamma. "I like morning calls."

Whomper waited awhile for a suitable tree to come floating nearer with its roots in the air. He caught hold of it with his tail and asked: "Anybody else coming?"

"Thanks, no," replied the mousewife. "That's not to my taste. Looks like a messy household."

"Nobody's invited me," said Misabel sullenly.

She saw Whomper put off. The tree trunk glided away. Suddenly Misabel felt very deserted and took a desperate jump. She managed to cling to the branches, and Whomper helped her aboard without comment.

Slowly they sailed on and landed at the verandah roof. They climbed in through the nearest window.

"Glad to meet you," said Moominpappa. "May I introduce: my wife; my son; the Snork Maiden; the Mymble's daughter; Little My."

"Misabel," said Misabel.

"Whomper," said Whomper.

"You're cracked!" said Little My.

"This is an introduction," explained the Mymble's

daughter. "You'd better keep quiet now, because this is a real visit."

"It's a bit untidy here today," said Moominmamma apologetically. "And I'm afraid the drawing-room's under water."

"Oh, don't mention it," replied Misabel. "What a splendid view you've got. And what wonderful weather we're having."

"Think so?" asked Whomper with some surprise.

Misabel blushed deeply. "I didn't mean to tell a fib," she said. "It just sounded so nice."

There was a pause.

"We're a bit crowded as it is," continued Moominmamma shyly. "Still, I think it's nice for a change. Do you know, I've been looking at my kitchen in quite a new way recently . . . especially when the chairs are upside-down. And how warm the water's become all of a sudden. We like swimming very much in our family."

"You do, do you," replied Misabel politely.

There was a pause again.

A faint trickling sound was heard.

"My!" said the Mymble's daughter sternly.

"It wasn't me," said Little My. "It's the sea coming in through our window."

She was right. The water was rising again. A ripple rolled over the window-sill. And then another.

Suddenly quite a breaker drenched the carpet.

The Mymble's daughter quickly pocketed her little sister and exclaimed: "What great luck that we like swimming so much in our family!"

CHAPTER III

About learning to live in a haunted house

Moominmamma was sitting on the roof with her handbag, work-basket, coffee pot, and the family photograph-album in her lap. Now and again she had to move a little higher away from the rising sea, as she didn't like to trail her tail in the water. Especially not when there were callers.

"We simply can't take the whole drawing-room suite," said Moominpappa.

"Dearest," replied Moominmamma. "What's the use of tables without chairs and chairs without tables? And of beds if there's no linen cupboard?"

"You're right," Moominpappa admitted.

"And a mirror-cabinet's very useful," said Moominmamma blandly. "You know yourself how nice it is to take a look in the glass in the morning. And," she continued after a while, "the couch is so nice for a quiet spell of thinking in the afternoon."

"No, not the couch," Moominpappa said determinedly.

"As you think best, dear," she replied.

Uprooted bushes and trees came floating along. Carts and kneading troughs, prams, fish-chests, landing-stages, and fences sailed on, empty or thronged with house-wrecked people. They were all too small, however, as rafts for a drawing-room suite.

But after a while Moominpappa pushed his hat back and looked sharply out over the sea. Something strange was on its way, carried by the inward current. Moominpappa had the sun straight in his eyes and couldn't tell if it was anything dangerous, but anyway it looked like a big thing, big enough to hold ten drawing-rooms and an even larger family than his.

Far out the thing had looked just like a large tin, ready to sink. Now it resembled a sea shell raised on edge.

Moominpappa turned to his family and remarked: "I think we'll manage."

"Of course we'll manage," replied Moominmamma. "We're only waiting for our new home. Only bad people fare badly."

"Not always," said Whomper. "I know villains who have never even fallen in the water."

"What a poor life," said Moominmamma, wonderingly.

Now the strange thing had drifted closer. It was quite clearly a kind of house. Two golden faces were painted on its roof; one was crying and the other one laughing at the Moomins. Beneath the grinning faces gaped a kind of large rounded cave filled with darkness and cobwebs. Obviously the great wave had carried away one of the walls of the house. On either side of the yawning gap drooped velvet curtains sadly trailing in the water.

Moominpappa stared in among the shadows.

"Anybody home?" he shouted cautiously.

No answer. They could hear an open door banging with the roll of the sea, and curls of dust scurried to and fro over the empty floor.

"I hope they were saved," said Moominmamma worriedly. "Poor family. I wonder what they looked like. It's really quite terrible to take their home away from them like this . . ."

"Dearest," said Moominpappa. "The water's rising."

"I know, I know," answered Moominmamma. "I suppose we'd better move over, then."

She climbed over to her new home and looked around her. These people had been just a little untidy, she could see. But then, who isn't. They had saved a lot of old disused things. Pity that the wall had fallen out, but now in summertime it wasn't so very important.

"Where'll we put the dining-room table?" asked Moomintroll.

"Here, in the middle of the floor," replied his mother. She felt very much more at ease when the beautiful drawing-room chairs with their dark-red plush and dangling tassels were assembled around her. The strange room became cosy at once, and Moominmamma happily seated herself in the rocking-chair and started to dream of curtains and sky-blue wallpaper.

"Now there's only the flag pole left above water," said Moominpappa sadly. Moominmamma patted his paw. "It was such a nice house," she replied. "Far better than this one. But after a while you'll see that everything feels just as usual."

(Dear reader, Moominmamma was totally wrong. Nothing was going to be quite as usual, because the house wasn't an ordinary house at all, nor had any ordinary family lived there. I won't tell you more now.)

"Shall I rescue the flag?" asked Whomper.

"No; leave it," said Moominpappa. "It looks so proud."

Slowly they drifted further up Moominvalley. When they arrived at the first pass to the Lonely Mountains they could still see the flag waving a merry farewell over the water.

★   ★   ★

Moominmamma had laid the table for supper in her new home.

The table looked a little lonely in the large and unfamiliar room. The chairs, the mirror-cabinet, and the linen cupboard kept watch around it, but behind them lurked an expanse of darkness, silence, and dust. The ceiling, from which the drawing-room lamp should have hung securely with its fringe of red tassels—the ceiling was the strangest of all. It was lost in mysterious, moving, and fluttering shadows, while something large and vague kept slowly rocking to and fro with the house's movements in the water.

"There's a lot of things one can't understand," Moominmamma said to herself. "But why should everything be exactly as one is used to having it?"

She counted the teacups on the table, and then she saw that they had forgotten to bring the marmalade over to their new home.

"What a shame," said Moominmamma. "As if I hadn't known that Moomintroll loves marmalade with his tea. How could I forget."

"Perhaps those people who lived here before also forgot to take their marmalade with them?" Whomper suggested helpfully. "Perhaps it was difficult to pack? Or if there was so little left in the pot it didn't matter?"

"Well, if one could find it," Moominmamma replied doubtfully.

"I'll have a look," said Whomper. "There must be a pantry somewhere."

He made his way into the darkness.

In the middle of the floor a door stood alone by itself. Whomper stepped through it just for form's sake and was surprised to find that it was made of plywood, and had a tiled stove painted on its backside. Then he ascended a staircase and found that it ended in mid-air.

"Somebody's pulling my leg," Whomper thought. "Only I don't think he's funny. A door should lead somewhere and a staircase, too. What would life be like if a Misabel suddenly behaved like a Mymble, or a Whomper like a Hemulen?"

Further on he found heaps of rubbish: curious frames of plaster, plywood, and canvas, evidently broken things that the former family hadn't cared to carry up to the attic or had started to make but never finished.

"What are you looking for?" asked the Mymble's daughter, coming out of a cupboard that had neither shelves nor back to it.

"Marmalade," replied Whomper.

"Seems to be all kinds of things here," said the Mymble's daughter, "so why not marmalade. It must have been a funny family."

"We saw one of them," said Little My importantly. "One who didn't want to be seen himself!"

"Where?" asked Whomper.

The Mymble's daughter pointed towards a dark corner where a lot of rubbish was piled up to the ceiling. A palm was leaning against the wall nearby and melancholically rustling its paper leaves.

"A villain!" whispered Little My. "Only waiting to knock us all over the head!"

"Now, take it easy," said Whomper with a slight catch in his throat.

He approached a little door that stood ajar and sniffed carefully.

It led to a narrow passage mysteriously winding on into darkness.

"I suppose the pantry would be somewhere in these parts," said Whomper.

They entered the passage and discovered that it

was lined with small doors. The Mymble's daughter peered at the nearest doorplate and spelled out the faded letters. "P, r, o, p, e, r, t, i, e, s," she read, "Properties. What a villainous name!"

Whomper braced himself and knocked. They waited, but evidently Mr. Properties wasn't in.

The Mymble's daughter pushed the door open.

Never before had they seen so many things at one time and in one place. The walls were all shelves up to the ceiling and down to the floor, and the shelves contained all the things that can be placed on shelves. Large bowls filled with fruit, playthings, table-lamps and china, tin helmets and flowers, tools and stuffed birds, books and telephones, fans and buckets, globes and guns, hatboxes and mantel clocks, and letter-scales and . . .

Little My took a flying jump from her sister's shoulder and landed on one of the shelves. She

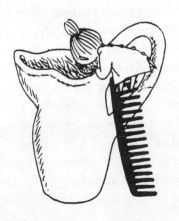

stared in a mirror and cried: "Look! I'm growing smaller all the time! I can't even see myself any more!"

"It's not a real looking-glass," explained the Mymble's daughter. "You're here all right, life-size."

Whomper hunted for marmalade. "Perhaps jam will do just as well," he said and tried to take the lid off a jam pot.

"Painted plaster," stated the Mymble's daughter. She took an apple and chewed at it. "Wood," she said.

Little My laughed.

But Whomper felt worried. All the things around him were false. Their pretty colours were a sham, and everything he touched was made of paper or wood or plaster. The golden crowns weren't nice and heavy, and the flowers were paper flowers. The fiddles had no strings and the boxes no bottoms, and the books couldn't even be opened.

Troubled in his honest heart, Whomper pondered over the meaning of it all, but he couldn't find any solution. "I wish I were just a tiny bit more clever," he thought. "Or a few weeks older."

"I like it here," said the Mymble's daughter. "It's just as if nothing really mattered here."

"Does anything matter anywhere?" asked Little My.

"No," her sister replied happily. "Don't ask such silly questions."

At that moment somebody gave a snort. Loudly and contemptuously.

They looked frightenedly at one another.

"I'm going back," Whomper mumbled. "All these things make me sad."

A loud thump resounded from the drawing-room, and a light cloud of dust rose from the shelves. Whomper snatched a sword and rushed out in the passage. They could hear Misabel squeaking.

The drawing-room was completely dark. Something large and yielding struck Whomper in the face. He closed his eyes and thrust his sword

straight through the invisible enemy. There was a sharp, rending sound, as if the enemy was made of cloth, and when Whomper dared to open his eyes again he could see daylight through the hole he had made.

"What are you doing?" asked the Mymble's daughter behind him.

"I've killed Properties," replied Whomper in a trembling voice.

The Mymble's daughter laughed and climbed through the hole into the drawing-room. "And what are *you* up to here?" she asked.

"Mother just pulled a rope!" cried Moomintroll.

"And then something terribly big fell down from the ceiling," cried Misabel.

"And all of a sudden we had a landscape in the room," said the Snork Maiden. "At first we thought it was real. Until you came in through the lawn."

The Mymble's daughter turned for a look.

She saw a wood of very green birches by a highly-coloured blue lake. Whomper's face was peering out of the grass with a relieved expression.

"Great goodness," Moominmamma said. "I thought it was some kind of curtain string. And then all this comes sailing down. What luck nobody was hurt. Did you find any marmalade?"

"No," answered Whomper.

"Well, we must have some tea in any case," said Moominmamma. "We can look at this picture meanwhile. It's wonderful. I hope it's going to stay where it is now."

She began pouring out tea.

And at that moment somebody laughed.

It was a spiteful laugh that sounded immensely old, and it emerged from the dark corner behind the paper palm.

"What are you laughing at?" asked Moominpappa after a long silence.

The silence only lengthened.

"Won't you take a cup of tea?" asked Moominmamma uncertainly.

The corner remained silent.

"It must be someone who has lived here before us," she said. "Why won't he step out and introduce himself?"

They waited a long time, but as nothing happened, Moominmamma said: "Your tea's getting cold, children," and began to share out the cheese in equal pieces. Then while she spread butter on the toast a sudden shower of rain drummed on the roof.

Just as suddenly a gale started to whine and whistle outside.

They looked out and saw the sun sinking peacefully in a summer sea, smooth as a mirror.

"Something rotten here," remarked Whomper. He seemed rather upset.

The gale heightened. They distinctly heard the sound of surf breaking on a distant shore, and the rain evidently continued to pour down over their heads—but outside, the weather looked just as lovely as before. And then the thunder started: at first a quiet rumbling in the distance. Then it drew closer, white lightning flashed through the drawing-room, and soon peal after peal rolled over the unhappy Moomins.

The sun was still setting, quietly and nicely.

Then the floor began to turn around. It started off on a slow pace, but soon it went faster and faster, until the tea splashed to and fro in the cups and spilled over the rims. The drawing-room behaved like a merry-go-round, and the table and chairs and all the Moomins and the mirror-cabinet and the linen cupboard could do nothing but hang on.

In a little while everything stopped as suddenly as it had started. Thunder, lightning, rain, and wind, all were gone.

"What a very strange world the world is," exclaimed Moominmamma.

"That wasn't real!" cried Whomper. "There were no clouds. And the lightning struck thrice and nothing broke! And the rain and wind and . . ."

"Somebody was *laughing* at me all the time!" said Misabel.

"It's all over now," said Moomintroll.

"We'll have to be very careful," said his father. "This is a dangerous, haunted house, and anything may happen." He looked around him with shining eyes.

"Thanks for the tea," said Whomper.* He walked to the edge of the drawing-room and stared out in the dusk. "They're all so very unlike me," he thought. "They have feelings and they see colours and hear sounds and whirl around, but *what* they feel and see and hear, and *why* they whirl, don't concern them in the least."

The uppermost rim of the sun-disc disappeared in the water. And at the same moment the whole drawing-room was splendidly lit.

In astonishment the Moomins looked up from their cups of tea. An arch of burning lamps, red and blue, stretched above them. It framed the

* Moomin people thank each other not only for tea but after every meal they eat together. They like to feel polite. *Translator.*

evening sea like a wreath of stars, beautiful and friendly-looking. A similar row of lamps glowed along the floor.

"That's to prevent people from falling in the water," said Moominmamma. "How orderly life can be. But all these exciting and wonderful events have made me just a little tired. I think I'll retire now."

But before Moominmamma pulled her counterpane over her nose she remembered to say: "Still, please wake me up if anything new happens!"

      ★   ★   ★

Later in the evening Misabel went for a solitary stroll by the sea. She saw the moon rise and start his lonesome journey through the night.

"He's exactly like me," Misabel thought sadly. "So plump and lonely."

At this thought she felt so forsaken and mild that she had to cry a little.

"What are you crying for?" asked Whomper nearby.

"I don't know, but it feels nice," replied Misabel.

"But people cry because they feel sorry, don't they?" objected Whomper.

"Well, yes—the moon," Misabel replied vaguely and blew her nose. "The moon and the night and all the sadness there is . . ."

"Oh, yes," said Whomper.

CHAPTER IV

About vanity and the dangers of sleeping in trees

A few days passed.

The Moomins were beginning to get used to their strange home. Every evening, exactly at sundown, the beautiful lamps were lighted. Moominpappa found out that the red velvet curtains could be pulled to against the rain, and that there was a small pantry under the floor. It had a round little roof and was quite cool, as there was water around it on three sides. But the nicest discovery was that the ceiling was filled with pictures, still more beautiful than the one with the birches. You could pull them down and back up again, just as you liked. There was one picture of a verandah with a fret-

49

work railing, and it became their favourite, because it reminded them of Moominvalley.

The whole family would have felt completely happy, had it not been for the strange laugh which sometimes cut them short when they talked with each other. At other times there were just contemptuous snorts. Somebody was snorting at them but never showed himself. Moominmamma used to fill a special bowl at the dinner-table and put it by the paper palm in the dark corner, and the following day the bowl was always carefully emptied.

"It's someone who is very shy," she said.

"It's someone who's *waiting*," said the Mymble's daughter.

*   *   *

One morning Misabel, the Mymble's daughter, and the Snork Maiden were combing their hair.

"Misabel ought to change her hair-do," remarked the Mymble's daughter. "A parting in the middle doesn't suit her."

"But no fringe for her," said the Snork Maiden and ruffled up her soft hair between the ears. She gave her tail-tuft a light brushing and turned her head to see if the fluff was tidy down her back.

"Does it feel nice to be fluffy all over?" asked the Mymble's daughter.

"Very," the Snork Maiden replied with satisfaction. "Misabel! Are *you* fluffy?"

Misabel didn't answer.

"Misabel ought to be fluffy," said the Mymble's daughter and began to tie her hair in a knot.

"Or curly all over," said the Snork Maiden.

All of a sudden Misabel stamped her feet. "You and your old fluff!" she cried out, bursting into tears. "You know everything, don't you! And the Snork Maiden hasn't even got a frock on! I'd never never show myself if I weren't properly dressed! I'd sooner be *dead* than have no frock on!"

Misabel hurried off across the drawing-room and into the passage. She stumbled sobbing through the dark, and then she stopped short and felt very much afraid. She had remembered the strange laugh.

Misabel stopped crying and anxiously began to feel her way back again. She fumbled and fumbled for the drawing-room door, and the longer she fumbled the more afraid she felt. Finally she found a door and pulled it open.

It wasn't the drawing-room at all. It was quite another room. A dimly-lighted room containing a long row of heads. Cut-off heads on long and narrow necks, with an unusual lot of hair. They were all looking towards the wall. "If they'd been looking at me," Misabel thought confusedly. "Imagine if they had been looking at me . . ."

She was so scared at first that she didn't dare to move a step. She could only stare, bewitched, at the golden curls, the black curls, the red curls . . .

★   ★   ★

Meanwhile the Snork Maiden was feeling rather sorry in the drawing-room.

"Never mind Misabel," said the Mymble's daughter. "Anything makes her fly off the handle."

"But she was right," the Snork Maiden mumbled with a glance down at her stomach. "I ought to have a frock."

"Of course not," said the Mymble's daughter. "Don't be silly."

"But you have one," protested the Snork Maiden.

"Well, that's me," said the Mymble's daughter carelessly. "Whomper! Should the Snork Maiden put on a frock?"

"If she's cold," replied Whomper.

"No, no, just anyway," explained the Snork Maiden.

"Or if it rains," said Whomper. "But then it's more sensible to put on a raincoat."

The Snork Maiden shook her head. For a while she hesitated. Then she said: "I'll go and have this matter out with Misabel." She went for a flashlight and stepped into the small passage. It was empty.

"Misabel?" cried the Snork Maiden in a hushed voice. "As a matter of fact, I like your parting in the middle . . ."

But no Misabel answered her. Then the Snork Maiden caught sight of a streak of light at one of the doors and pattered up to it to look through the crack.

In the room behind the door Misabel was sitting all alone. She had wholly new hair on. Long, yellow corkscrew curls framed her worried face.

The little Misabel stared at her reflection in the glass and sighed. She reached for another beautiful mop of hair, a red and wild one, and pulled the fringe down to her eyes.

It didn't make matters better. Finally, with trembling paws, she seized a set of curls that she had laid aside because she loved them most. They were magnificently jet-black with little dashes of gold glittering like tears. Breathlessly Misabel fitted this splendid hair over her own. For a long minute she looked at herself in the mirror. Then she lifted off the hair very slowly and sat staring at the floor.

The Snork Maiden slipped back without disturbing her. She realized that Misabel wanted to be alone.

But the Snork Maiden didn't return to the others. She went instead a bit further along the passage, sniffing the air. She had noticed an enticing and very interesting scent, a scent of face powder. The small round spot from her flashlight wandered along the walls and finally caught the magic word "Costumes" on a door. "Dresses," whispered the Snork Maiden to herself. "Frocks!" She turned the door-handle and stepped in.

"Oh, how wonderful," she panted. "Oh, how beautiful!"

Robes, dresses, frocks. They hung in endless rows, in hundreds, one beside the other all round the room—gleaming brocade, fluffy clouds of tulle and swansdown, flowery silk, night-black velvet with glittering spangles everywhere like small, many-coloured blinker beacons.

The Snork Maiden drew closer, overwhelmed. She fingered the dresses. She seized an armful of them and pressed them to her nose, to her heart. The frocks rustled and swished, they smelled of dust and old perfume, they buried her in rich softness. Suddenly the Snork Maiden released them all and stood on her head for a few minutes.

"To calm myself," she whispered. "I'll have to calm down a bit. Or else I'll burst with happiness. There's too many of them . . ."

*   *   *

A little before dinner Misabel was back again in the drawing-room and sat grieving alone by herself in a corner.

"Hello," said the Snork Maiden and sat down by her side.

Misabel gave her a glance without replying.

"I've been looking for a dress," said the Snork Maiden. "And I found several hundred and was so happy."

Misabel made a sound that could have meant anything.

"Perhaps a thousand!" continued the Snork Maiden. "And I looked and looked and tried on one after the other and felt sadder and sadder."

"Did you!" Misabel exclaimed.

"Yes, what d'you think," said the Snork Maiden. "They were far too many, you see. I couldn't ever have had them all or even choose the prettiest. They nearly made me afraid! If there'd been only two instead!"

"That would have been much easier," replied Misabel a little more cheerfully.

"So in the end I just ran away from them all," finished the Snork Maiden.

They sat silent for a while and watched Moominmamma lay the table.

"Just think," said the Snork Maiden, "just think what sort of a family lived here before us! A thousand frocks! A floor that goes around sometimes, pictures hanging from the ceiling, all their belongings on shelves in Mr. Properties' room. Paper doors and a special rain. What can they have looked like?"

Misabel thought of the beautiful curls and sighed.

But behind Misabel and the Snork Maiden, behind the dusty rubbish by the paper palm, gleamed a pair of observant and sharp little eyes. The eyes looked at them with some disdain and then wandered over the drawing-room suite to rest at last upon Moominmamma, who was now bringing in a large dish of porridge. The eyes sharpened still more, and the nose between them wrinkled with a noiseless snort.

"Dinner, please, everybody!" cried Moominmamma. She filled a plate with porridge and set it on the floor by the palm.

The Moomins came running and sat down to dinner. "Mother," began Moomintroll and reached for the sugar, "don't you think . . ." and then he stopped short and dropped the sugar bowl with a thump back on the table. "Look!" he whispered. *"Look!"*

They turned around and looked.

A shadow detached itself from the dark corner. A grey and wrinkly shape came shuffling out, blinked in the sun, shook its whiskers, and gave the company a hostile look.

"I'm Emma," said the old stage rat solemnly, "and I'd like to tell you that I hate porridge. This is the third day you're eating porridge."

"We're having gruel tomorrow," Moomin-mamma replied shyly.

"I loathe gruel," answered Emma.

"Won't Emma take a chair, please," said Moo-minpappa. "We thought this house was deserted, and that's why we—"

"House, indeed," Emma interrupted with a snort. "This is no *house*." She limped up to the table but didn't sit down."

"Is she angry at me?" whispered Misabel.

"What have you done?" asked the Mymble's daughter.

"Nothing," Misabel mumbled to her plate. "I just feel as if I had done something. I always feel as if someone were angry with me. If I were the won-derfulest Misabel in the world everything would be different . . ."

"Well, but as you aren't," replied the Mymble's daughter and continued her meal.

"Was Emma's family saved?" asked Moomin-mamma sympathetically.

Emma didn't answer. She was looking at the cheese . . . She reached for the cheese and put it in her pocket. Her gaze roved on and fastened on a small piece of pancake.

"That's ours!" cried Little My, and landed on the pancake with a flying leap.

"That wasn't nice manners," said the Mymble's daughter reproachfully. She lifted her sister aside, brushed some dust off the pancake, and hid it under the tablecloth.

"Whomper dear," Moominmamma hastened to say. "Run along, and look if we have something nice for Emma in the pantry!"

Whomper hurried off.

"Pantry!" exclaimed Emma. "The pantry, indeed! You seem to believe that the prompter's box is a pantry! And the stage a drawing-room, with the drops for pictures! And the curtain's just curtains and the properties a person!" She had become quite red in the face, and her nose was wrinkled up to her forehead. "Really, thank goodness," she cried, "thank goodness that my beloved husband, Stage Manager Fillyjonk (mayherestinpeace), can't see you all! You don't know a thing about the theatre, that's clear, less than nothing, not even the shadow of a thing!"

"There was a herring, but it's rather an old one," said Whomper, returning.

Emma fiercely struck the fish from his hand and shuffled stiffly back to her corner. For a long time she kept rattling a number of things and finally pulled out a large broom and began to sweep the floor.

"What's a theatre?" Moominmamma whispered uneasily.

"I don't know," replied Moominpappa. "Looks as if one ought to know it."

★   ★   ★

In the evening a strong scent of rowan-tree flowers crept into the drawing-room. Birds came fluttering in to hunt for spiders in the ceiling, and Little My met a big and dangerous ant on the rug. They had landed in a forest without anybody noticing.

The general excitement was great. All forgot to

be afraid of Emma and gathered talking and ges-
ticulating by the water.

They made fast the house to a big rowan tree.
Moominpappa fastened the hawser to his walking-
stick and pushed the stick through the pantry roof.

"Don't you damage the prompter's box!" Emma
shouted at him. "*Is* this a theatre or a landing-
stage?"

"I suppose it's a theatre if Emma says so," Moominpappa replied humbly. "But none of us quite
knows what that means."

Emma stared at him without replying. She shook
her head, shrugged her shoulders, gave a strong
snort, and continued to sweep the floor.

Moominpappa was looking up into the top of
the large tree. Swarms of bumblebees were hum-
ming around the white flowers. The bole was nicely
curved, forming a kind of rounded fork, exactly
suited to sleep in if you were small enough.

"I'll sleep in this tree tonight," said Moomintroll
suddenly.

"I, too," said the Snork Maiden at once.

"And me!" shouted Little My.

"We're sleeping at home," said the Mymble's daughter. "There might be ants in the tree, and if they bite you you'll swell up and grow bigger than an orange."

"But I want to grow up. Iwanttogrowupiwant-togrowup!" cried Little My.

"You'd better be good now," said her sister. "Or else the Groke will get you."

Moomintroll was still looking up at the green ceiling of leaves. It was a little like home in Moominvalley. He began whistling to himself while he planned the rope-ladder he intended to make.

Emma came running. "Stop whistling at once!" she cried.

"Why?" asked Moomintroll.

"It's disaster to whistle on the stage," Emma replied in a lowered voice. "You don't even know that." Mumbling and shaking her broom, she limped off into the shadows. The Moomins looked after her a little uneasily. Then they forgot it all.

*   *   *

At bedtime Moomintroll was hoisting up bed-clothes into the tree. Moominmamma was packing a small breakfast basket for Moomintroll and the Snork Maiden. It would be fun to have it when they awakened the next morning.

Misabel looked on.

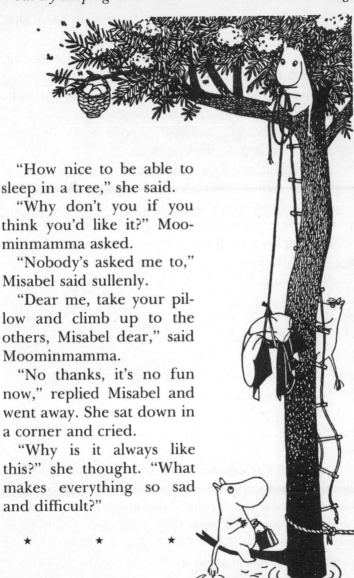

"How nice to be able to sleep in a tree," she said.

"Why don't you if you think you'd like it?" Moominmamma asked.

"Nobody's asked me to," Misabel said sullenly.

"Dear me, take your pillow and climb up to the others, Misabel dear," said Moominmamma.

"No thanks, it's no fun now," replied Misabel and went away. She sat down in a corner and cried.

"Why is it always like this?" she thought. "What makes everything so sad and difficult?"

★　　　★　　　★

Moominmamma lay awake for a long time that night.

She listened to the water lapping beneath the floor and felt a bit uneasy. She could hear Emma shuffling along the walls, muttering to herself. Unknown animals were shrieking in the forest.

"Moominpappa," she whispered.

"Mm," replied Moominpappa.

"I feel a bit anxious about something."

"Don't bother, everything's all right," mumbled Moominpappa and slept on.

Moominmamma lay looking into the forest for a while. But little by little she drowsed off, and night fell over the drawing-room.

★   ★   ★

An hour passed.

Then a grey shadow crept over the floor and stopped at the pantry. It was Emma. Mustering all her aged strength and anger, she managed to pull Moominpappa's stick out of the hole in the pantry roof. She threw stick and hawser far away out in the water.

"Spoiling the prompter's box!" she muttered to herself, emptied a bowl of sugar from the supper table into her pocket, and returned to her corner.

Freed from its moorings, the house started off with the current. For a while the twinkling arch of red and blue lamps glittered among the trees.

Then it disappeared, and only the greyish moonlight lighted the forest.

CHAPTER V

About the consequences of whistling on the stage

The Snork Maiden awoke shivering with cold. Her fringe felt quite damp. Large curtains of fog were drifting in between the trees and shutting them off behind pale grey walls. The tree trunks were damp and black as coal, but the moss and lichens on them had become light and formed delicate rose-patterns everywhere.

The Snork Maiden buried her head in the pillow and tried to continue her nice dream. She had dreamt that her nose was very small and wonderful, but now she couldn't catch the dream again.

66

And suddenly she felt that there was something amiss.

With a start she looked around her.

Trees and fog and water. But no house. The house was gone, and they were all alone. For a moment the Snork Maiden was dumbfounded.

Then she leant down and gave Moomintroll a slight shake.

"Protect me," she whispered, "protect me, dear!"

"Is that some new game?" Moomintroll asked sleepily.

"No, it's real," said the Snork Maiden and looked at him, her eyes black with alarm.

They could hear the fog drearily dripping around them, blip, blip, in the black water. All the flower petals had fallen off during the night. It was a cold morning.

They sat side by side for a long time without moving. The Snork Maiden cried silently into her pillow.

At last Moomintroll rose and mechanically lifted down the breakfast basket from its branch.

It was filled with neat little sandwich-packs wrapped in wax paper, two of each kind. He laid them out in a row but didn't feel a bit hungry.

Suddenly Moomintroll noticed that his mother had written something on the sandwich wrappers. There was a label on each pack, like "Cheese" or "Just butter" or "Dear sausage" or "Good morning!" On the last package she had written "This Is from

Pappa." It contained the tin of lobster that Moominpappa had saved ever since spring.

And all of a sudden Moomintroll had a feeling that the situation wasn't so very perilous.

"Now, don't you cry, dear, and try to eat your sandwiches," he said. "We'll climb further through the forest. And please comb your fringe a little, because I like to see you beautiful!"

★   ★   ★

Moomintroll and the Snork Maiden spent the whole day climbing from tree to tree. Evening had already come when they saw the first green moss gleam greenly through the water, slowly slanting upwards and forming a solid shore.

Oh, how good to tread on firm ground again and burrow your paws in soft honest moss! The forest was spruce. All around them cuckoos were cuckooing in the silent and windless evening, and swarms of midges were dancing beneath the dense spruces. (Happily, midges cannot bite through Moomin fur.)

Moomintroll stretched himself out in the moss. He felt dizzy from looking down into the swirling, restless water so long.

"I'm making believe that you've kidnapped me," whispered the Snork Maiden.

"So I have," replied Moomintroll kindly. "You howled terribly, but I kidnapped you all right."

The sun had set, but now in June there was of course no darkness at night to speak of. The night was pale and dreamy and full of magic.

Deep beneath the spruces a spark lit up and kindled a small fire. It was a miniature bonfire of spruce needles and twigs, and they could clearly see a lot of tiny forest-people trying to roll a whole cone into the fire.

"They've a Midsummer fire," exclaimed the Snork Maiden.

"Yes," said Moomintroll with a sigh. "We'd forgotten that it's Midsummer Eve."

A wave of homesickness passed through them. They arose from the moss and wandered deeper into the forest.

At this time of the year Moominpappa's palm-wine used to ripen back home in Moominvalley. Down by the shore the big Midsummer bonfire was lighted, and all the people from the valley and the woods gathered to admire it. Other fires were burning further along the shore and out on the islands, but the Moominvalley fire used to be the biggest. When the flames rose at their highest Moomintroll used to wade out in the warm water and lie on his back floating on the swell and looking at the fire.

"It was reflected in the sea," said Moomintroll.

"Yes," said the Snork Maiden. "And when it had burnt down we went off to pick nine kinds of flowers and put them under our pillow and then our dreams came true. But you weren't allowed to say a word while you picked them, nor afterwards until morning."

"Did your dreams come true?" asked Moomintroll.

"Of course," said the Snork Maiden. "And always nice things."

They had reached a glade in the forest. A fine mist filled it like milk in a bowl.

Moomintroll and the Snork Maiden stopped

anxiously at the edge of the wood. Through the mist they could dimly see a small house with fresh leaf garlands around its chimney and gateposts.

In the mist, or in the house, a small bell was tinkling. Then all became silent—then the jingle came again. But there was no smoke from the chimney, and the window was dark.

★   ★   ★

While all this happened, the morning aboard the floating house had been a most miserable one. Moominmamma declined to eat. She sat in the rocking-chair, repeating over and over: "Poor little children, my poor dear little Moominchild! All alone in a tree! He'll never find his way home again. Just think when night comes and the owls begin to screech!"

"They won't do that until August," Whomper comforted her.

"Well, anyway," said Moominmamma, weeping still. "There's always something or other screeching."

Moominpappa stared sadly at the hole in the pantry roof. "It's all my fault," he said.

"You mustn't say that," said Moominmamma. "Your stick must have been old and rotten and whoever could know that? And I'm quite sure they'll find their way back again soon. I really am!"

"If they aren't eaten up," said Little My. "If the ants haven't bitten them, so they're bigger than oranges already."

"Run along and play now, or you'll get no dessert," said the Mymble's daughter.

Misabel changed into a black dress. She sat down in a corner and had a good cry all by herself.

"Are you really taking it so hard?" asked Whomper sympathetically.

"No, just a little less," replied Misabel. "But I'm taking the chance to have a cry over a lot of things now when there's a good reason."

"Oh, yes," replied Whomper without quite understanding.

He tried to figure out the cause of the accident. He examined the hole in the pantry roof and all of the drawing-room floor. The only thing he found was a trap-door under the carpet. It opened straight down on the black, lapping water

under the house. Whomper was very interested.

"Perhaps that's a kind of dust-chute," he said. "Or a swimming-pool. If it isn't for throwing one's enemies in?"

But nobody else took any interest in his trap-door. Only Little My laid herself on her stomach to look down into the water. "I suppose it's for enemies," she said. "A splendid trap-door for big and small villains!"

She lay there all day looking for villains, but she unfortunately didn't find any.

*   *   *

No one reproached Whomper afterwards.

It happened just before dinner.

Emma hadn't turned up at all during the day and didn't even show herself at dinner-time.

"Perhaps she's ill," said Moominmamma.

"Not she!" said the Mymble's daughter. "She's only pinched enough sugar now so she can *live* on it."

"Dear, run along and look to see if she's all right," Moominmamma said tiredly.

The Mymble's daughter went over to Emma's corner and asked: "Moominmamma's compliments, and have you got a stomach-ache from all the sugar?"

Emma's whiskers bristled. But before she found a suitable reply the whole house rattled with a tremendous shock and leant dangerously over.

Whomper came scuttling along the floor in an avalanche of dinner china, and most of the pictures fluttered down from the ceiling, burying the drawing-room.

"We've run aground!" cried Moominpappa, half stifled beneath the velvet curtains.

"My!" shouted the Mymble's daughter. "Where's my sister?"

But Little My couldn't have told her even if she had wanted to, for once. She had rolled straight through the trap-door, down into the black water.

Suddenly a horrible chuckle filled the drawing-room. It was Emma's bitter laugh.

"Ha, ha!" she laughed. "There you are now! That'll teach you not to whistle on the stage!"

CHAPTER VI

About revenge on Park Keepers

If Little My had been only slightly bigger, who knows if she wouldn't have drowned. Now she bobbed light as a bubble through the whirls of water and, snorting and spitting, popped her head above the surface again. She floated like a cork and was swiftly carried away by the current.

"This is fun," said Little My to herself. "My sister's going to wonder." She looked around her and discovered Moominmamma's cake-tin and work-basket afloat quite near. After some hesitation (because she knew there were still a few cakes left) she chose the work-basket and clambered aboard it.

She had a nice long time examining everything
in it and cutting up a couple of skeins. Then she
curled up in the angora wool and went to sleep.

The work-basket sailed on. The house had gone
aground in the middle of an inlet, and now the
basket drifted shorewards, where, in among the
reeds, it finally stopped in the mud. This didn't
wake Little My, who had always been a sound
sleeper. She didn't awake at first even when a
fishing-hook came flying and caught in the work-
basket. There was a jerk when the line tightened
and was slowly pulled home.

Dear reader, prepare for a surprise. Chance and
coincidence are strange things. Without knowing
anything of each other and each other's business
the Moomin family and Snufkin had happened to
arrive at the same little inlet on Midsummer Eve.
It was Snufkin himself in his old green hat who
now stood on the shore and stared at the work-
basket he had caught.

"By my hat, if it isn't a small Mymble," he said
and took the pipe from his mouth. He then poked
at Little My with the crochet hook and said kindly:
"Don't be afraid!"

"I'm not even afraid of ants," replied Little My
and sat up.

They looked at each other.

The last time they had met, Little My had been
so small as to be nearly invisible, so it wasn't very
strange that they didn't recognize each other now.

"Well, well, dear child," remarked Snufkin and scratched his head.

"Well, yourself, with knobs on," said Little My.

Snufkin sighed. He was here on important business, and he had really hoped to be alone for a few days more before returning to Moominvalley for the summer. And then some careless Mymble went and put her child to sea in a work-basket. Just for the fun of it.

"Where's Mother?" he asked.

"Somebody ate her," replied Little My untruthfully. "Have you any food?"

Snufkin pointed with his pipe-stem. A small kettle of peas was simmering over his camp-fire nearby. Beside it stood another with hot coffee.

"But I suppose milk's what you drink," he said.

Little My gave a contemptuous laugh. She did not bat an eyelid as she swallowed two brimming teaspoonfuls of coffee and ate no fewer than four peas.

Then Snufkin carefully extinguished his camp-fire with water and remarked: "Well?"

"Now I want to sleep some more," said Little My. "I always sleep best in pockets."

"Quite," said Snufkin and pocketed her. "The main thing in life is to know your own mind." He tucked in the angora wool around her.

Then Snufkin continued his way across the meadows by the shore.

The great flood wave had never reached as far

as the inlet. Here summer was as it had always been. Nothing was known about the volcanic eruption, even if Snufkin had often wondered at the splendidly red sunsets, and the ashes drifting with the wind, of late. He knew nothing at all about the things that had happened to his friends in Moominvalley, and he supposed that they had at this moment gathered on their verandah for the usual quiet Midsummer celebration.

Hc had thought sometimes of Moomintroll, who was probably waiting for him to return. But first he had to settle his account with the Park Keeper. And that could be done only on Midsummer Eve.

Tomorrow all would be over.

Snufkin produced his mouth-organ and began to play his and Moomintroll's old song, "All small beasts should have bows in their tails."

Little My awoke at once and put out her head.

"I know that one," she cried. And then she sang in her shrill and gnat-like voice:

"All small beasts should have bows in their tails
 Because now the Hemulens are closing the jails:
 Whomper'll dance to the moon and rejoice.
 Blow your nose, little Misabel, and laugh at the
     noise!
 Look at the tulips, how happy and bright
 They're shining in morning's wonderful light!
 Slowly, oh, slowly a heavenly night
 Is fading away like an echoing voice!"

"Wherever can you have heard that one?" Snufkin asked in some surprise. "You sang it nearly right. You're a strange child."

"You're dead right there, pal," said Little My. "And I've got a secret, too."

"A secret?"

"You bet, a secret. About a thunderstorm that isn't a thunderstorm and a drawing-room that turns about. But I won't tell you more than that!"

"I've got a secret, too," said Snufkin. "In my knapsack. I'll show it to you after a while. Because I'm going to settle an old account I have with a villain!"

"Big or small?" asked Little My.

"Small," said Snufkin.

"That's good," said Little My. "Small villains are much better. They break more easily."

She crawled happily down into her angora wool again, and Snufkin continued his walk. He had arrived at a long fence. It was hung with notices at regular intervals:

ABSOLUTELY
NO ADMITTANCE

The Park Keeper and the Park Wardress lived together, in the park, of course. They had cut and sheared every single one of the trees into round blobs and square cubes, and all the gravel paths were straight as pointers. As soon as any leaf of grass dared to come up, it was cut off and had to start struggling over again.

The lawns were fenced in on all sides, and the fences were hung with notices telling in big black letters that something or other was not allowed.

Into this horrible park came every day twenty-four small subdued children who had for some reason become forgotten or lost. They were furry woodies who liked the park as little as the sand-box where they were told to play. What they wanted was to climb trees, stand on their heads, run across the lawns . . .

Neither the Park Keeper nor the Park Wardress could understand this. They sat watching the woodies, one on each side of the sand-box. What could the little children do?

★　　　★　　　★

To this park came Snufkin with Little My in his pocket. He crept silently along the fence, looking in at his old enemy, the Park Keeper.

"What are you going to do to him?" asked Little My. "Hang him, boil him, or stuff him?"

"Scare him!" replied Snufkin and clenched his teeth around the pipe-stem. "There's only one person in the whole world whom I really dislike, and that's the Park Keeper. I'm going to pull down all his notices about forbidden things."

Snufkin now rummaged in his knapsack and pulled out a large paper bag. It was full of small, glossy white seeds.

"What's that?" asked Little My.

"Hattifattener seed," answered Snufkin.

"Oh," said Little My, astonished. "Do Hattifatteners come from seeds?"

"They do," said Snufkin. "But the important thing is: only if the seeds are sown on Midsummer Eve."

He began throwing handfuls of seed between the fence rails. He crept noiselessly along the whole of the park fence and scattered his seeds everywhere, but was careful to throw them sparsely, so that the Hattifatteners wouldn't have their paws entangled when they came up. When Snufkin's bag was empty he sat down, lit his pipe, and waited.

The sun was setting, but the evening was warm, and the Hattifatteners began to grow at once. Here and there on the neatly mowed lawn round white blobs were appearing, like snowball mushrooms.

"Look at that one," said Snufkin. "In a little while it'll have its eyes over the earth."

He was right. Very shortly two round eyes appeared beneath the white skull.

"They're specially electric when new-grown," explained Snufkin. "Look now, he's got his paws!"

The air was already filled with a faint rustling sound from all the growing Hattifatteners. The

Park Keeper still hadn't noticed anything unusual, because he was keeping a keen eye on the little woodies. But on the lawns all around him Hattifatteners were shooting up in hundreds. They had scarcely more than their feet left in the ground. Soon they would take their first steps. A smell of sulphur and burnt rubber drifted through the park. The Park Wardress sniffed.

"What's that smell?" she asked. "Children, who of you's smelling?"

Faint electric shocks were noticeable in the ground.

The Park Keeper began to shift his feet uneasily. His shining metal buttons were flashing small blue sparks.

All of a sudden the Park Wardress gave a cry and jumped up on the seat of her chair. She pointed a shaking finger at the lawn.

The Hattifatteners had grown to life-size and now came swarming and moiling towards the Park Keeper from all directions, attracted by his electrified buttons. Small flashes of lightning crossed the air, and the buttons were crackling. Suddenly the Park Keeper's ears lit up. Then his hair crackled and sparkled, his nose began to glow—and all of a sudden the Park Keeper was luminous from top to toe! Shining like a full moon, he scuttled off towards the park gates, followed by the army of Hattifatteners.

The Park Wardress was already climbing the

fence. Only the little children were left. They sat quietly in the sand-box and looked very surprised.

"Smart," said Little My, impressed.

"And that's that!" said Snufkin, pushing back his hat. "And now we'll pull down every single notice, and every single leaf of grass shall be allowed to grow as it likes to."

All his life Snufkin had longed to pull down notices that asked him not to do things he liked to do, and he was fairly trembling with excitement and expectation. He started off with

NO SMOKING

Then he flew at

DO NOT SIT ON THE GRASS

After that he turned on

LAUGHING AND WHISTLING
STRICTLY PROHIBITED

and the next minute

NO HOP, NO SKIP,
AND DEFINITELY NO JUMP
ALLOWED HERE

followed suit.

The little woodies stared at him with more and more astonishment.

Little by little it was dawning on them that he had come to their rescue. They left the sand-box and gathered around him.

"Go home, little ones," said Snufkin. "Go wherever you please."

But they did not go, they followed him everywhere. When the last of the notices was trampled to earth and Snufkin lifted his knapsack on to his back, they still followed at his heels.

"Shoo, little ones," said Snufkin. "Run along to mamma now."

"Perhaps they have no mamma," said Little My.

"But I'm not a bit used to children!" said the now terrified Snufkin. "I don't even know if I like them!"

"They seem to like you," replied Little My, grinning broadly.

Snufkin looked at the silently admiring group that had flocked around his legs.

"As if one weren't enough," he said. "Well. Come along, then. But don't blame me if everything goes wrong!"

And with twenty-four serious little children at his heels Snufkin wandered off over the meadows, bleakly wondering what he would do when they got hungry, had wet feet, or a stomach-ache.

CHAPTER VII

About the dangers of Midsummer Night

At half-past ten on Midsummer Eve, at the moment when Snufkin was busy building a hut of spruce twigs for his twenty-four little children, Moomintroll and the Snork Maiden stood listening in another part of the wood.

The bell that had tinkled in the mist was silent again. The forest was asleep, and the black and empty window-panes of the little house in the glade stared sadly at them.

But inside, a Fillyjonk was sitting, listening to the ticking of her clock and the passing of the time. Now and then she went over to the window and looked out into the fair June night, and every time she moved, there was a little tinkle from the jingle bell she carried on the tassel of her cap. This used to cheer up the Fillyjonk (that was why she had sewn it on), but tonight it only made her sadder. She sighed and wandered around, sat down, and got up again.

She had laid the table with three plates and glasses and a vase of flowers, and on her stove was a pancake grown coal-black from waiting.

The Fillyjonk looked at her clock, and at the garlands over the door, and at herself in the mirror on the wall—and then she buried her head in her arms on the table, and began to cry. Her cap slipped forward with a single melancholy, jingling plunk, and her tears rolled slowly down on to her empty plate.

It isn't always easy being a Fillyjonk.

At that moment somebody knocked.

The Fillyjonk gave a start, jumped to her feet, blew her nose, and opened the door.

"Oh," she said, disappointedly.

"Merry Midsummer!" said the Snork Maiden.

"Thanks, the same to you," replied the Fillyjonk confusedly. "Nice of you to wish me that."

"Well, we just stopped to ask if you've seen any new house, I mean theatre, hereabouts," said Moomintroll.

"Theatre?" repeated the Fillyjonk suspiciously. "No, quite the contrary—I mean, not at all."

There was a slight pause.

"In that case, I suppose we'll be going," said Moomintroll. "Thanks all the same."

The Snork Maiden looked at the laid table and the garlands by the door. "Have a nice party," she said genially.

At these words the Fillyjonk's face wrinkled up, and she began crying once more.

"There'll be no party," she sobbed. "The pancake has dried up, and the flowers are fading, and the clock just ticks, and nobody comes. They won't come this year either! They've got no family feeling!"

"Who isn't coming?" Moomintroll asked sympathetically.

"My uncle and his wife!" cried the Fillyjonk. "I keep sending them an invitation card for every Midsummer Eve, and they never come."

"Why don't you ask somebody else, then?" said Moomintroll.

"I've got no other relatives," explained the Fillyjonk. "And of course it's one's duty to ask one's relatives to dinner on holidays."

"So you don't like it, really?" asked the Snork Maiden.

"Of course not," replied the Fillyjonk tiredly and sank down by the table. "My uncle and aunt aren't very nice people."

Moomintroll and the Snork Maiden sat down beside her.

"Perhaps they don't like it either?" said the Snork

Maiden. "I suppose you couldn't ask us, who are nice, instead?"

"What are you saying?" said the Fillyjonk, surprised.

It was evident that she was thinking hard. Suddenly the tassel on her cap rose a bit in the air, and the jingle bell gave a merry tinkle.

"As a matter of fact," she said slowly, "there's really no need to ask them, as none of us likes it?"

"Absolutely no need," said the Snork Maiden.

"And nobody's hurt if I ask anyone I like? Even if they're no relatives of mine?"

"Definitely not," Moomintroll assured her.

The Fillyjonk beamed with relief. "Was it that easy?" she exclaimed. "Oh, what a relief! Now we'll celebrate the first happy Midsummer I've ever had, and how we shall celebrate! Please, please let's have something really exciting!"

★   ★   ★

And this Midsummer was to be far more exciting than the Fillyjonk could hope for.

"Here's to Pappa and Mamma!" said Moomintroll and drained his glass. (And at that very moment Moominpappa was sitting aboard the theatre and raising his glass towards the night outside in a toast for his son. "To Moomintroll, and may his return be happy," he said solemnly. "To the Snork Maiden and Little My!")

Everybody was satisfied and happy.

"And now for the Midsummer fire," said the Fillyjonk. She blew out the lamp and put the matches in her pocket.

Outside, the sky was still quite light, and you could make out every single leaf of grass on the ground. Behind the spruce tops, where the sun had gone to rest for a while, a streak of red light remained waiting for the new day.

They wandered through the deeply silent wood and came out on the meadows by the shore, where the night was fairer still.

"A strange smell the flowers have tonight," remarked the Fillyjonk.

A faint odour of burnt rubber was drifting over the ground. The grass crackled electrically when they trod on it.

"That's the Hattifattener smell," replied Moomintroll with some surprise. "I thought they were out on the sea at this time of the year."

The Snork Maiden stumbled over something. " 'Do not tread on the grass,' " she read. "Look," she said, "here's a lot of notices that somebody's thrown away!"

"How wonderful, everything's allowed!" cried the Fillyjonk. "What a night! Let's build our bonfire of the notices! And dance round it until they've burned to ashes!"

★   ★   ★

Their Midsummer bonfire was burning brightly. With merry cracklings it consumed the stack of useless notices: "No Singing on the Premises," "Do Not Touch the Flowers," and "Sitting on the Grass Allowed on Special Request Only" . . . Showers of sparks spurted up against the pale night sky, and a dense smoke billowed out over the meadows and remained floating in the air like woolly white curtains.

The Fillyjonk was singing. She danced on thin legs around the bonfire and poked at the embers with a stick.

"Never more my uncle," she sang. "And never more my aunt. I'll never ask them any more! I don't, I won't, I shan't!"

Moomintroll and the Snork Maiden were sitting side by side and looking contentedly into the fire.

"What do you suppose my mamma is doing now?" asked Moomintroll.

"Celebrating, of course," said the Snork Maiden.

The pile of notices collapsed in a shower of sparks. The Fillyjonk cheered.

"I'll be feeling sleepy soon," said Moomintroll. "Did you say nine kinds of flowers?"

"Yes, nine kinds," said the Snork Maiden. "And you must promise not to speak a word until morning."

Moomintroll nodded solemnly. He then performed a lot of gestures that meant: "Good night, see you again tomorrow," and shuffled off through the dewy grass.

"I want to gather flowers, too," said the Fillyjonk. She came scuttling, sooty and happy, out of the smoke. "I like magic tricks! Do you know any other ones?"

"I know a very creepy Midsummer Magic," whispered the Snork Maiden. "But it's unspeakably horrible."

"I dare anything tonight," said the Fillyjonk with a reckless tinkle.

The Snork Maiden looked around her. Then she leant forward and whispered in the Fillyjonk's outstretched ear: "First you must turn seven times around yourself, mumbling a little and stamping your feet. Then you go backwards to a well, and turn around, and look down in it. And then, down in the water, you'll see the person you're going to marry!"

"And how do you get him up from there?" asked the Fillyjonk excitedly.

"Oh, no, no, it's his *face* you see," explained the Snork Maiden. "His ghost! But first we must gather the nine kinds of flowers. One, two, three, and now if you say a word you'll never marry!"

★   ★   ★

While the fire slowly died down to a glow and
the morning breeze lazily drifted over the grass,
the Snork Maiden and the Fillyjonk gathered their
secret nosegays. Time and again they caught each
other's eye and laughed, because that wasn't forbidden.

Then they came to the well.

The Fillyjonk waggled her ears.

The Snork Maiden nodded, a little pale.

They began to growl in a low voice, to stamp
their feet and turn around. Five times, six times.
The seventh turn took some time, because now
they felt quite frightened. But once you have started
a Midsummer Magic you have to go through with
it, otherwise anything may happen.

With fast-beating hearts they walked backwards
to the well, and stopped.

The Snork Maiden took a firm hold of the
Fillyjonk's paw.

The streak of sunlight on the eastern sky was
broadening, and the smoke of the bonfire was
turning pink.

Together, at the same time, they turned and
looked down the well.

They saw their own reflections, they saw the rim
of the well and the reddening sky.

They waited, trembling. Long.

And suddenly—well, this is almost too terrible—
suddenly they saw a large head appear beside their
own reflections.

The head of a Hemulen!

An angry and very ugly Hemulen in a policeman's cap.

At the moment Moomintroll pulled his ninth
flower from the ground he heard a terrible shouting. As he turned he saw a big Hemulen who was
holding the Snork Maiden with one paw and the
Fillyjonk with the other and shaking them roughly.

"Come along, all three of you!" cried the Hemulen. "You grokely pyromaniacs! Deny if you can
that you've pulled down all the notices and burned
them! Deny it if you can!"

But of course they couldn't. They had promised
not to utter a word.

CHAPTER VIII

About how to write a play

Just fancy if Moominmamma had known that Moomintroll was in jail when she awoke on Midsummer Day! And if anybody had been able to tell the Mymble's daughter that her little sister was asleep in Snufkin's spruce-twig hut, snugly curled up in angora wool!

Now they were ignorant, but full of hope. Hadn't they been mixed up before in stranger events than any other family they knew of, and hadn't everything turned out for the best every time?

"Little My is used to taking care of herself,"

said the Mymble's daughter. "I'm more worried about the people that happen to cross her path."

Moominmamma looked out. It was raining.

"I hope they won't get colds," she thought and carefully sat up in bed. It was necessary to move with care, because since they had run aground, the floor was sloping so strongly that Moominpappa had thought it best to nail all the furniture to the floor. The meals were a bother, because the plates kept sliding off the table, and nearly always cracked if you tried to nail them down. Most of the time the Moomins felt like mountaineers. As they had to walk continually with one leg a little higher up than the other, Moominpappa had begun to worry about their legs growing uneven. But Whomper was of the opinion that everything would even out if they took care to walk in both directions.

Emma was sweeping as usual.

She clambered laboriously up the floor, pushing the broom before her. When she was halfway all the dust went rolling back, and she had to start all over again.

"Wouldn't it be more practical to sweep the other way?" Moominmamma suggested helpfully.

"Nobody's going to teach me how to sweep floors," replied Emma. "I've done this floor in this direction ever since I married Mr. Fillyjonk, and I'm going to do it this way till I die."

"Where's Mr. Fillyjonk?" asked Moominmamma.

"He's dead," answered Emma with dignity. "The

fire curtain came down on his head one day, and they both cracked."

"Oh, poor, poor Emma!" cried Moominmamma.

Emma dug a yellowed portrait from her pocket. "This is Mr. Fillyjonk as a young man," she said.

Moominmamma looked at the photograph. Mr. Fillyjonk, the stage manager, was sitting in front of a picture with palms. He had impressive whiskers. At his side stood a young person of worried appearance with a small cap on her head.

"What a stylish gentleman," said Moominmamma. "I've seen that picture he has behind him."

"Back-drop for *Cleopatra*," said Emma coldly.

"Is the young lady's name Cleopatra?" asked Moominmamma.

Emma clasped her forehead with her free paw. "*Cleopatra* is the title of a play," she said snappily. "And the young lady by Mr. Fillyjonk's side is his affected niece. A most disagreeable niece! She keeps sending us invitation cards for Midsummer every year, but I'm very careful not to reply. She just wants to get into the theatre, I'm sure."

"And why won't you answer her?" Moominmamma asked reproachfully.

Emma put her broom aside.

"I've had about enough," she declared. "You know nothing about the theatre, not the least bit. Less than nothing, and that's that."

FOTO J:SON

To my dear Emma

"But if Emma would only be so kind as to explain a little to me," said Moominmamma shyly.

Emma hesitated, and then she resolved to be kind.

She seated herself at Moominmamma's bedside and began: "A theatre, that's no drawing-room, nor is it a house on a raft. A theatre is the most important sort of house in the world, because that's where people are shown what they could be if they wanted, and what they'd like to be if they dared to, and what they really are."

"A reformatory," said Moominmamma, astonished.

Emma patiently shook her head. She took a scrap of paper, and then with a trembling paw drew a picture of a theatre for Moominmamma. She explained every detail and wrote down the explanations so that Moominmamma wouldn't forget them. (You'll find the picture here somewhere.)

While Emma sat drawing, all the others flocked around her.

"I'll tell you about when we performed *Cleopatra*," Emma was saying. "The house was full (I'll explain that if you wait), and the audience dead silent, because it was the first night. I had turned on the footlights and floats (perhaps you'll understand), at sundown as usual, and the moment before the curtain rose I thumped the floor thrice with my broom-handle. Like this!"

"Why?" asked the Mymble's daughter.

"For effect," replied Emma, her small eyes gleaming. "Fate knocking, don't you see. Well, then the curtain rises. There's a red spot on Cleopatra—"

"She wasn't ill, was she?" asked Moominmamma.

"That means a red light, a spotlight," said Emma with hard-won composure. "All the people in the house catch their breath—"

"Was Mr. Properties there?" Whomper asked.

"Properties are not a person, as you seem to believe," explained Emma quietly. "They are all the things you need for acting ... Well, our leading lady was really lovely, a dark-haired beauty—"

"Leading lady?" Misabel interrupted her.

"Yes, the most important of all the actresses. She who has the nicest part and always gets what she wants. But goodness gracious what—"

"I want to be a leading lady," said Misabel. "But I'd want sad parts. With lots of shouting and crying and crying."

"In a tragedy, then, a real drama," said Emma. "And you'd have to die in the final act."

"Yes," cried Misabel, her cheeks glowing. "Oh, to be someone really different! Nobody would say 'Look, there's old Misabel' any more. They'd say 'Look at that pale lady in red velvet ... the great actress, you know ... She must have suffered much.'"

"Are you going to play for us?" asked Whomper.

"I? Play? For you?" whispered Misabel with tears starting to her eyes.

"I want to be a leading lady, too," said the Mymble's daughter.

"And what play would you perform?" asked Emma sceptically.

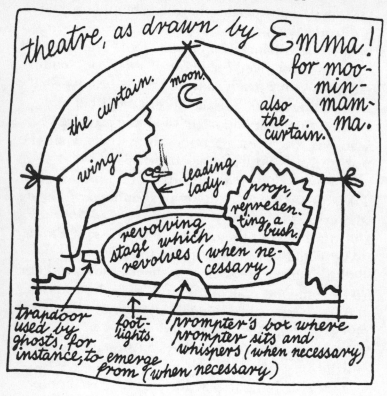

theatre, as drawn by Emma! for moo-min-mam-ma.

the curtain.

moon.

also the curtain.

wing.

leading lady.

prop, represen-ting a bush.

revolving stage which revolves (when ne-cessary)

trapdoor used by ghosts, for instance, to emerge from (when necessary)

foot-lights.

prompter's box where prompter sits and whispers (when necessary)

Moominmamma looked at Moominpappa. "I suppose you could write a play if Emma helped you," she said. "You've written your Memoirs, and it can't be so very hard to put in a few rhymes."

"Dear me, I couldn't write a play," replied Moominpappa, blushing.

"Of course you could, dear," said Moominmamma. "And then we all learn it by heart, and everybody comes to look at us when we perform it. Lots of people, more and more every time, and they all tell their friends about it and how good it is, and in the end Moomintroll will hear about it also and find his way back to us again. Everybody comes home again and all will be well!" Moominmamma finished and clapped her paws together.

They looked doubtfully at each other. Then they glanced at Emma.

She extended her paws and shrugged her shoulders. "I expect it'll be gruesome," she said. "But if you absolutely *want* to get the raspberry, as we say on the stage, well, I can always give you a few hints about how to do it correctly. When I can find the time."

And Emma sat down and began to tell them more about the theatre.

★　　　★　　　★

In the evening Moominpappa had finished his play and proceeded to read it to the others. No one interrupted him, and when he had finished there was complete silence.

Finally Emma said: "No. Nono. No and no again."

"Was it that bad?" asked Moominpappa, downcast.

"Worse," said Emma. "Listen to this:

    "I'm not afraid of any lion,
      Be it a wild 'un or a shy 'un.

That's horrid."

"I want a lion in the play, at all costs," Moominpappa replied sourly.

"But you must write it again, in blank verse! Blank verse! Rhymes won't do!" said Emma.

"What do you mean, blank verse?" asked Moominpappa.

"It should go like this: Ti-dum, ti-umty-um—ti-dumty-um-tum," explained Emma. "And you mustn't express yourself so naturally."

Moominpappa brightened. "Do you mean: 'I tremble not before the Desert King, be he a savage beast or not so savage'?" he asked.

"That's more like it," said Emma. "Now go and write it all in blank verse. And remember that in all the good old tragedies most of the people are each other's relatives."

"But how can they be angry at each other if they're of the same family?" Moominmamma asked cautiously. "And is there no princess in the play? Can't you put in a happy end? It's so sad when people die."

"This *is* a tragedy, dearest," said Moominpappa. "And because of that, somebody has to die in the end. Preferably all except one of them, and perhaps that one, too. Emma's said so."

"Bags I to die in the end," said Misabel.

"And can I be the one who fixes her?" asked the Mymble's daughter.

"I thought Moominpappa would write a mystery," Whomper said disappointedly. "Something with a lot of suspects and nasty clues."

Moominpappa arose pointedly and collected his papers. "If you don't like my play, then by all means write a better one yourselves," he remarked.

"Dearest one," said Moominmamma. "We think it's wonderful. Don't we?"

"Of course," everybody said.

"You hear," said Moominmamma. "Everybody likes it. If you just change the style and the plot a little. I'll see to it that you're not disturbed, and you can take the whole bowl of candy with you."

"All right, then," replied Moominpappa. "But there must be a lion."

"Of course there must be a lion, dear," said Moominmamma.

Moominpappa worked hard. Nobody spoke or moved. As soon as one sheet of paper was filled he read it aloud amid general applause. Moominmamma refilled the bowl at regular intervals. Everybody felt excited and expectant.

Sleep was hard to find that evening for them all.

Emma felt her old legs come to life. She could think of nothing but the dress rehearsal.

CHAPTER IX

About an unhappy daddy

On the morning of the day Moominpappa wrote
his play and Moomintroll was jailed, Snufkin was
awakened by a trickle of rain seeping through the
roof of his spruce-twig hut. He looked out into the
wet forest, very carefully, because he didn't want
to wake up the twenty-four little children.

He looked out on a carpet of white flowers that
shone like little stars among glistening green ferns.
He wished bitterly that they had all been turnips
instead.

"I suppose that's the way fathers think," he
thought. "What shall I give them to eat today?

Little My won't need many beans, but all these others are going to finish off my provisions in no time."

He turned and glanced at the woodies asleep in the moss.

"And now they'll catch cold from the rain, I expect," he mumbled bleakly to himself. "And that won't be the worst. I simply *can't* invent anything new to amuse them. They don't smoke. My stories scare them. And I can't stand on my head all day, because then I won't get to Moominvalley until summer's over. What a blessing it's going to be when Moominmamma takes care of them all!"

"Good old Moomintroll," Snufkin thought with sudden devotion. "We'll go for moonlight swims together again, and sit and talk in the cave afterwards . . ."

At that moment one of the woodies had a bad dream and began to cry. All the others awoke and cried too, out of sympathy.

"Wellwellwell," said Snufkin, "hoppityhoppity-hop! A Tweedledeedledeedledee!"

It had no effect.

"They didn't think you were funny," Little My explained. "You must do as my sister does. Tell them that if they don't shut up you're going to whack them silly. Then you ask them to forgive you and give them candy."

"And does that help?" Snufkin asked.

"No," said Little My.

Snufkin raised the spruce-twig hut from the ground and threw it into the bushes.

"That's what we do with a house when we've slept in it," he said.

The woodies fell silent at once and wrinkled their noses in the drizzle.

"It's raining," said a small woody.

"I'm hungry," said another.

Snufkin looked helplessly at Little My.

"Scare them with the Groke!" she suggested. "That's what my sister used to do."

"Does it make you a good girl?" asked Snufkin.

"Of course not!" said Little My and laughed so she toppled over.

Snufkin sighed. "Come along, come along," he said. "Get up, get up! Hurry up and I'll show you something!"

"What?" asked the woodies.

"Something . . ." said Snufkin uncertainly and waved his hands.

"You'll never manage this in your life," said Little My.

★   ★   ★

They walked and they walked.

And it rained and rained.

The woodies sneezed and lost their shoes and asked why they couldn't have some bread and butter. A few of them started a fight. One rammed his nose full of spruce needles, and another one got pricked by a hedgehog.

Snufkin came near to feeling sorry for the Park Wardress. He was now carrying one woody on his hat, two on his shoulders, and two more under his arms. Drenched and unhappy, he stumbled along through the blueberry scrub.

At that moment, that most melancholy moment, they arrived at a glade. And in the middle of the glade was a small house with withered garlands around its chimneystack and gateposts. Snufkin staggered to the door on wobbly legs. He knocked and waited.

Nobody opened.

He knocked once more. Nothing. Then he pushed the door open and stepped in.

Nobody was home. The flowers on the table were faded, the clock had stopped. He put down the woodies and went across the floor to the cold stove. There had been a pancake once. He went to look for a pantry. The woodies silently followed him with their eyes.

A moment of suspense followed. Then Snufkin returned with a whole keg of beans and put it on the table. "Now you can eat yourselves square and round again on beans," he said. "Because we're going to stay here a little while and calm down until I've learned your names. Light my pipe, someone!"

All the woodies rushed to light his pipe.

A while later there was a good fire in the stove, and all dresses and skirts and trousers were hung up to dry. A large dish of steaming beans stood on the table, and outside, the rain was gushing down from an evenly grey sky.

They listened to the rain scuttling over the roof and the logs crackling in the stove.

"Well, what about it, eh?" Snufkin asked. "Who wants to go back to the sand-box?"

The woodies looked at him and laughed. Then they started on the Fillyjonk's brown beans.

But the Fillyjonk was, as we know, quite unaware that she had guests, because she was already in jail for disorderly behaviour.

CHAPTER X

About the dress rehearsal

It was the day of the dress rehearsal of Moomin-pappa's play, and all the footlights were burning, although it was still only afternoon.

The beavers had been promised free tickets for the first night the following day if they would push the theatre back on an even keel, and now it was almost right, but the stage still slanted a little, which made the acting slightly strained.

The curtain was drawn, red and mysterious, and outside on the water a small flotilla of boats was curiously bobbing. They had waited since sunrise, and the people in them had brought their own dinners with them in paper bags, because dress rehearsals always take a lot of time.

"Mother, what's a dress rehearsal?" asked a poor hedgehog child in one of the boats.

"It's when they practise the play for the very last time to be quite sure that everything's in order," explained the hedgehog mother. "Tomorrow they'll act in real earnest, and then one has to pay to look at them. Today's free for poor hedgehogs like us."

But the people behind the curtain were not at all sure that everything was in order. Moominpappa was rewriting his play. Misabel was crying.

"Didn't we *tell* you that we both wanted to die in the end!" exclaimed the Mymble's daughter. "Why should only she be eaten by the lion? The Lion's Brides, we told you. Don't you remember?"

"All right, all right," Moominpappa answered nervously. "The lion shall devour, first you, and lastly Misabel. Don't disturb me, I'm trying to think in blank verse."

"Have you got the family matters right now, dear?" Moominmamma asked worriedly. "Yesterday the Mymble's daughter was married to your runaway son. Is it Misabel who's married to him now, and am I her mother? And is the Mymble's daughter unmarried?"

"I don't want to be unmarried," the Mymble's daughter said at once.

"They can be sisters," cried Moominpappa desperately. "The Mymble's daughter is your daughter-in-law. I mean mine. Your aunt, that is."

"I doubt it," remarked Whomper. "If Moominmamma's married to you, then it's *impossible* for your daughter-in-law to be our aunt."

"It's all the same to me," cried Moominpappa. "There'll never be any play to perform, anyway!"

"Easy now, easy now," said Emma with unexpected understanding. "Everything's going to be all right. And anyway the audience won't understand a word."

"Emma dear," said Moominmamma. "This dress is too narrow for me . . . it keeps slipping up in the back."

"Now remember," said Emma, her mouth full of pins, "you mustn't look so happy when you come on the stage and tell him that your son has told him a pack of lies!"

"No, I promise," said Moominmamma.

Misabel was reading her part. Suddenly she threw the paper away and cried: "It's far too lighthearted! It doesn't suit me at all!"

"Hush, Misabel," said Emma sternly. "We start now. Are the spots ready?"

Whomper turned on the yellow spotlight.

"Red! Red!" the Mymble's daughter shouted.

"My entrance's red! Why must he always turn on the wrong light!"

"They all do," said Emma calmly. "Are you ready?"

"I can't remember my lines," mumbled Moominpappa, panic-stricken. "Not a word!"

Emma patted him on the shoulder. "That's as it should be," she said. "Everything's exactly as it should be on a dress rehearsal."

She thumped the floor three times with her broomstick, and silence fell over the boats outside. With a thrill of happiness in her old body she grasped the crank handle to raise the curtain.

Admiring whispers were heard among the sparse audience. Most of the hedgehogs had never been to the theatre before.

They saw a landscape of wild rocks, in red light.

To the right of the mirror-cabinet (draped in black cloth), the Mymble's daughter was sitting, dressed in a tulle skirt and a wreath of paper flowers around her hairknot.

She studied the audience with great interest for some time and then spoke, rapidly and casually:

"If I must die tonight, in blooming youth,
  While all my innocence cries to high heav'n,
  Then into Blood may bloodily turn the sea
  And into dust the sprightliness of spring!
  A Rosebud, blushing still from childish sleep,
  I'm slewn to earth by unrelenting Fate!"

Behind the scenes rose a shrill chant. It was Emma:

"O Night, O Night, O Night, O Night of Fate!"

Now Moominpappa entered from the left with a cloak carelessly draped over his shoulder, turned to the audience, and recited in a trembling voice:

"The bonds of Family and Friendship must
Be broken at the sad command of Duty.
Alas, shall then my crown be lifted off
By th' sister of my daughter's nephew?"

He felt that there was something wrong with the words, and resumed:

"Alas, shall then my crown be lifted off
By the sister-in-law of my daughter's son?"

Moominmamma put in her head from the wings and whispered: "By the sister of my daughter's sister's son!"

"I know, I know," said Moominpappa. "I'll skip that part this time."

He took a step towards the Mymble's daughter, who hid herself behind the cabinet, and continued:

"Then tremble, treacherous Mymble, tremble
   now
 And listen to the beastly lion's roar
 As hungrily he stamps about his cage
 Ululating at the moon!"

A long silence followed.

"Ululating at the moon!" repeated Moominpappa, louder.

Nothing happened.

He turned to the left and asked: "Why doesn't the lion ululate?"

"I wasn't to ululate until Whomper hoisted the moon," replied Emma.

Whomper put out his head. "Misabel promised to make a moon, and she hasn't," he said.

"All right, all right," said Moominpappa hastily. "We'll try Misabel's entrance now, because I'm not in the right mood anyway."

Slowly Misabel glided on to the stage in her red velvet robe. For a long time she remained motion-less with her paw over her eyes, feeling what it felt like to be a leading lady. It felt wonderful.

"O happiness," prompted Moominmamma, who thought she had forgotten her opening lines.

"I know, I'm just holding them spellbound!" Misabel hissed back. She staggered towards the footlights and reached out her arms to the audience. There was a click as Whomper started the wind machine behind the scenes.

"Is that a vacuum-cleaner?" asked the hedgehog child.

"Hush!" said the hedgehog mother.

Misabel started on her first great monologue:

"O happiness and joy when I behold
  Yourself beheaded at my own behest . . ."

She took a rapid step, stumbled on the velvet train, and fell over the footlights straight down into the nearest hedgehog's boat.

The audience cheered and jointly lifted Misabel back up on the stage.

"Take my advice, miss," said a middle-aged beaver, "better cut off her head at once!"

"Whose head?" Misabel asked, wonderingly.

"Your son-in-law's niece's, of course," replied the beaver encouragingly.

"They've misunderstood the whole thing," whispered Moominpappa to Moominmamma. "Come on at once, please."

Moominmamma hastily gathered her skirts and appeared on the stage with a friendly and slightly shy smile.

"Now hide your face, I bring black tidings hither!
 Your son has told you but a pack of fibs!"

she said happily.

Moominpappa stared nervously at her.

"Where is the lion," she prompted helpfully.

"Where is the lion," repeated Moominpappa. "Where is the lion," he said uncertainly once more. Finally, he shouted: "Well, where is it?"

A great stamping could be heard behind the scenes. Then the lion entered. It consisted of a beaver in the forelegs and another in the hind legs. The audience shouted with delight.

The lion hesitated. Then it walked up to the footlights and took a bow, and broke in the middle.

The audience clapped and began to row home.

"It isn't finished!" shouted Moominpappa.

"Dearest, they'll come back tomorrow," said Moominmamma. "And Emma says that the first night never succeeds if the dress rehearsal hasn't been a little so-so."

"Does she really," replied Moominpappa, reassured. "Well, anyway they laughed several times!" he added happily.

But Misabel turned her back to the others for a while to quieten her thumping heart.

"They clapped!" she whispered to herself. "Oh, how happy I am! I'll always, always feel happy after this!"

CHAPTER XI

About tricking jailers

Next morning the playbills were sent out. All kinds
of birds flew along the inlet and dropped them.
The bills (written and coloured by Whomper and
the Mymble's daughter) fluttered down over the
forest and the shore and the meadows, in the water,
on housetops, and in gardens.

One of the playbills was dropped over the jail
and landed at the feet of the Hemulen, who was
sitting half asleep in the sunshine with his policeman's cap over his snout.

He picked it up, feeling very excited, and sus-
pecting a secret message intended for his prisoners.

At the moment he had not fewer than three
prisoners, the most he had ever had since he took

his jailer's degree. It was nearly two years since the last time he had locked anybody up, so naturally he took no chances now.

The Hemulen adjusted his glasses and read the bill aloud to himself:

First Night ! ! !
THE LION'S BRIDES or BLOOD WILL OUT
A Tragedy in One Act by Moominpappa
Performed by
Moominpappa, Moominmamma, the Mymble's
Daughter, Misabel, and Whomper
Chorus: Emma
Tickets against anything eatable
The Tragedy begins at sunset if the weather keeps good, and will end at ordinary bedtime. Performed in the middle of Spruce Creek. Boats for hire from the Hemulens
The Management

"A play?" said the Hemulen thoughtfully and took off his glasses again. Deep in his heart stirred a faint, un-Hemulic memory of his childhood. His aunt had taken him to the theatre once. That was something about a princess who went to sleep in a rosebush. It had been very beautiful. The Hemulen had rather liked it.

Suddenly he knew that he wanted to go to the theatre again.

But who would guard his prisoners?

He knew of no Hemulen who could possibly find the time. The poor jailer racked his Hemulic brain. He pressed his snout against the iron bars of the cage that stood in the shadow beside his chair, and said: "I'd like so much to go to the theatre tonight."

"The theatre?" said Moomintroll, pointing his ears.

"Yes, *The Lion's Brides*," explained the Hemulen and pushed the playbill between the bars. "And now I can't imagine whom I could get to watch you in the meantime."

Moomintroll and the Snork Maiden read the playbill. They looked at each other.

"I suppose it's about some princess or other," said the Hemulen plaintively. "It's ages since I saw a little princess."

"Of course you'll have to go," said the Snork Maiden. "Is there really no one who could watch us?"

"Well, there's my cousin," replied the Hemulen. "But she's too kindhearted. Perhaps she'd let you out."

"When are we going to be beheaded?" the Fillyjonk suddenly asked.

"Oh, dear me, nobody's going to behead you," replied the Hemulen, quite embarrassedly. "You'll just have to sit there until you confess. Then you'll be sentenced to painting new notices and writing

out 'Strictly forbidden' five thousand times each."

"But we're innocent," began the Fillyjonk.

"Yes, I know," said the Hemulen. "I've heard it before. They all say that."

"Listen," said Moomintroll. "You'll be sorry for the rest of your life if you don't go to that play. I'm certain there are princesses in it. *The Lion's Brides.*"

The Hemulen shrugged his shoulders with a sigh.

"Now don't be foolish," said the Snork Maiden entreatingly. "Let's have a look at your cousin. I suppose a kindhearted jailer is better than none, anyway!"

"Perhaps," replied the Hemulen sourly. He rose and shuffled off through the bushes.

"There you are!" said Moomintroll. "Remember our dream on Midsummer Night? About lions! A big lion that was bitten in the leg by Little My! But I wonder what they *are* up to at home!"

"I dreamed that I had a lot of new relatives," said the Fillyjonk. "Wasn't that horrid? Now, when I'm rid of the old ones."

The Hemulen returned. He was accompanied by a very small and thin Hemulen with a timid look.

"Do you think you can watch these for me?" he asked.

"Do they bite?" the small Hemulen whispered. She was evidently quite a failure (from a Hemulic point of view). The Hemulen snorted and gave her the key.

"Certainly," he said. "They'll bite your head off, snip-snop, if you let them out. Cheerio, I'm off to dress for the first night."

As soon as he had disappeared, the little Hemulen seated herself and began crocheting. Now and then she glanced at the cage. She looked frightened.

"What are you making?" the Snork Maiden asked kindly.

The small Hemulen gave a start. "I don't know, really," she whispered anxiously. "I just feel a bit more secure with my crocheting."

"Couldn't you make it into slippers? It's such a nice slipper colour," suggested the Snork Maiden.

The small Hemulen examined her crocheting and thought for a while.

"Don't you know anybody who has cold feet?" asked the Fillyjonk.

"Yes, I've got a girl friend," said the little Hemulen.

"I know one, too," the Fillyjonk continued in a friendly tone. "My aunt. She's working at a theatre. There's such a cross-draught, they say. Must be an unpleasant place."

"There's quite a draught here, too," said Moomintroll.

"My cousin ought to have thought of that," said the little Hemulen shyly. "If you wait a bit I'll crochet slippers for you."

"I suppose we'll be dead before they're finished," Moomintroll replied bleakly.

The little Hemulen looked quite alarmed and came nearer to the cage. "Suppose I put a blanket over it?" she suggested.

Moomintroll and the Snork Maiden shrugged their shoulders and huddled shivering close to each other.

"Do you really feel such a draught?" asked the little Hemulen worriedly.

The Snork Maiden coughed hollowly. "*Perhaps* a cup of tea with black currant jam would save me," she said. "Possibly."

The little Hemulen hesitated. She was pressing her crocheting to her snout and staring at them. "If you died . . . " she said in a trembling voice. "If you died, then there wouldn't be any fun left for my cousin when he comes home."

"Probably not," said the Fillyjonk.

"And anyway I have to measure your feet for the slippers."

They nodded convincingly.

Then the little Hemulen opened the cage and said, shyly: "Perhaps you'll give me the pleasure of accepting a nice cup of hot tea? With black currant jam. And of course you shall have the slippers as soon as I can crochet them. So kind of you to hit upon that slipper idea! It'll make my crocheting so purposeful, if you see what I mean."

They walked to the little Hemulen's house and had some tea. She insisted on baking several sorts of cake, so that it was already dusk when the Snork

Maiden rose and said: "Now I'm afraid we'll have to go. Thank you ever so much for the nice party!"

"It's really terrible to have to put you back in jail again," the little Hemulen said apologetically and lifted down the key from its nail.

"But we don't intend to go back there," replied Moomintroll. "We're going home to the theatre."

The little Hemulen had tears in her eyes. "That'll make my cousin terribly, terribly disappointed," she said.

"But we're absolutely innocent!" the Fillyjonk exclaimed.

"Oh, why didn't you tell me that at once," said

the little Hemulen, relieved. "Then of course you must go home. But perhaps I'd better come along with you and explain it all to my cousin."

CHAPTER XII

About a dramatic first night

While the little Hemulen entertained her guests at tea, more and more of the playbills kept fluttering down over the forest. One of them drifted down in a small glade and landed and stuck on a newly-tarred roof.

The twenty-four small woodies immediately swarmed up on the roof to bring down the bill. Every one of them wanted to be the one who gave it to Snufkin, and as the paper was rather thin it was quickly transformed into twenty-four very small playbills (of which a few fell down the chimney and caught fire).

"A letter for you!" shouted the woodies, gliding, scuttling, and rolling down from the roof.

"Oh, you Grokelings!" said Snufkin, who was busy washing socks by the porch. "Have you forgotten that we tarred the roof this morning? Do you want me to go away and leave you, throw myself in the sea, or box your ears?"

"No!" shouted the woodies, pulling at his coat. "We want you to read your letter!"

"My letters, you mean," replied Snufkin and brushed off the soap-suds from his hands in the hair of the nearest little child. "Well, well. Looks like it might have been an interesting one."

He smoothed out the crumpled scraps on the lawn and tried to piece them together.

"Aloud!" cried the woodies.

"Tragedy in One Act," Snufkin read. "*The Lion's Brides* or . . . (here's a piece missing) Tickets against anything eatable . . . (mphm) . . . begins at suns . . . (sunset) . . . if the weather keeps good (that's quite clear) . . . nary bedt . . . (no, I can't make that out) . . . middle of Spruce Creek."

"Mphm," said Snufkin. "This, dear little beasts, is no letter at all—it's a playbill. Somebody seems to be producing a play tonight in Spruce Creek. Why it has to be in the water goodness knows, but perhaps it's needed for the plot."

"Are children allowed?" asked the smallest of the woodies.

"Are there real lions?" cried the others. "When do we go?"

Snufkin looked at them and understood that it was necessary to take them to the play.

"Perhaps I can pay for the tickets with the keg of beans," he thought worriedly. "If it's enough. We've eaten quite a lot . . . I hope people won't think that all twenty-four are my own . . . I'd feel embarrassed. And *what* shall I give them to eat tomorrow?"

"Aren't you happy to go to the theatre?" asked the smallest woody and rubbed his nose against Snufkin's trouser leg.

"Terribly happy, silk muzzle," replied Snufkin. "And now we'll try to clean you up. A little, at least. Have you any handkerchiefs? Because this is a tragedy."

They hadn't any.

"Well," said Snufkin. "You'll have to blow your noses in your petticoats. Or whatever you've got."

★   ★   ★

The sun was nearly at the horizon when Snufkin

had done with all the trousers and dresses. Of course, there was a certain amount of tar left, but at least it was evident that he had done his utmost.

Very excited and solemn, they started for Spruce Creek.

Snufkin led the way, carrying the keg of beans, and at his heels followed all the woodies by pairs, everyone with his or her hair neatly parted in the middle from the eyebrows all the way down to the tail.

Little My sat on Snufkin's hat, singing loudly. She had swathed herself in a kettle-holder, because there was likely to be a chill in the air later in the night.

Down at the shore the general excitement over the first night was already quite noticeable. The inlet was swarming with boats on their way out to the theatre. On a raft beneath the splendidly radiant footlights the Hemulic Voluntary Brass Band was playing and in full swing. Otherwise it was a calm and pleasant evening.

Snufkin hired a boat for two pawfuls of beans and set his course towards the floating theatre.

"Nufkin!" said the biggest of the woodies when they were half-way.

"Yes," said Snufkin.

"We've got a present for you," said the woody, blushing terribly.

Snufkin rested his oars and took the pipe from his mouth.

The woody extracted a crumpled thing of an indefinite colour from behind his back. "It's a tobacco pouch," he said indistinctly. "We've all of us taken turns to embroider it and didn't tell you a word!"

Snufkin received his present and peered into it (it was one of the Fillyjonk's old caps). He sniffed at it.

"It's raspberry leaves to smoke on Sundays!" the smallest woody shouted proudly.

"This is a splendid tobacco pouch," said Snufkin approvingly. "And the tobacco will be excellent for Sunday smoking."

He shook paws with all the woodies and thanked them.

"I haven't embroidered on it," Little My said from his hatbrim. "But the idea was mine!"

The rowing-boat was nearing the footlights, and Little My wrinkled her nose in some astonishment. "Are all theatres alike?" she asked.

"I think so," said Snufkin. "Now, when the fun starts they'll pull away those curtains, and then you must remember to be quite silent. Don't fall in the water if something awful happens. And after it's finished you clap your paws to show that you've liked it."

The woodies sat quite still and stared at everything.

Snufkin looked around him carefully, but nobody was laughing at them. Everybody looked at the lighted curtain. Only an elderly Hemulen came rowing up and said: "Admittance, please."

Snufkin raised his keg of beans.

"Do you pay for them all?" asked the Hemulen and began to count the children.

"Isn't it enough?" asked Snufkin, uneasily.

"Oh, yes, there's always a reduction in these cases," said the Hemulen and filled his bailer with beans from the keg.

Now the band stopped, and everybody clapped.

Then silence.

Three strong thumps sounded behind the curtain.

"I'm afraid," the smallest woody whispered. He was pulling at Snufkin's sleeve.

"Hold on and you'll be all right," said Snufkin. "Look, there goes the curtain."

The rocky landscape lay before the breathless spectators.

On the right the Mymble's daughter was sitting, dressed in tulle and paper flowers.

Little My leant down over the hatbrim and exclaimed: "Boil me if it isn't my old sister."

"Is the Mymble's daughter your sister?" asked Snufkin, surprised.

"I've been talking and talking about my sister, haven't I?" said Little My in a bored voice. "Haven't you listened at all?"

Snufkin stared at the stage. His pipe went out, but he forgot to light it. He saw Moominpappa enter from the left and declaim something peculiar about a lot of his relatives and a lion.

Suddenly Little My jumped down in his lap and said agitatedly: "Why is he angry at my sister? He has no *right* to scold my sister!"

"Sh! dear, it's only a play," replied Snufkin absentmindedly.

He now saw a small fat lady in red velvet enter to tell the audience that she was extremely happy. At the same time she seemed to have an ache somewhere.

Somebody else whom he didn't know kept shouting "O Night of Fate" behind the scenes.

Wondering more and more, Snufkin saw Moominmamma appear on the stage. "What's up with the whole family?" he thought. "I know they've always had ideas, but this! I suppose Moomintroll is the next to jump in and begin reciting."

But Moomintroll didn't come. Instead a lion entered and roared.

The woodies began to cry and nearly turned the boat over.

"This is silly," remarked a Hemulen in a policeman's cap who was sitting in the next boat. "It's not a bit like that wonderful play I saw when I was young. About a princess who slept in a rosebush. I can't understand a word of what they mean."

"Theretherethere," said Snufkin to his panic-stricken woodies. "That lion's made out of an old counterpane."

But they didn't believe him. They saw quite clearly that the lion was chasing the Mymble's daughter all over the stage. Little My was shrilling like a whistle. "Save my sister!" she shouted. "Brain that lion!"

And suddenly she took a desperate leap up on the stage, rushed at the lion, and sank her small sharp teeth in its right hind leg.

The lion uttered an exclamation and broke in the middle.

The spectators now saw the Mymble's daughter lifting Little My in her arms and getting kissed on the nose, and they noticed that nobody spoke in blank verse any longer, but quite naturally. This met with general approval, because now it was finally possible to understand what the play was about.

It was about someone who had floated away from home, and had awful experiences, and now found her way home again. And everybody was marvelously happy and going to have a cup of tea.

"They're playing a lot better now, I think," said the Hemulen.

Snufkin began to hoist all his woodies up on to the stage. "Hello, Moominmamma!" he cried happily. "Can you take care of these for me?"

The play became funnier and funnier. By and by, the whole of the audience came climbing up on the stage and took part in the plot by beginning to eat the entrance fees that were laid out on the dining-room table. Moominmamma freed herself from the troublesome skirts and rushed to and fro handing out teacups.

The band started on the Hemulic Triumphal March.

Moominpappa was radiant with the great success, and Misabel was every bit as happy as at the dress rehearsal.

Suddenly Moominmamma stopped in the middle of the stage and dropped a teacup to the floor.

"Here he comes," she whispered, and everybody became silent.

Out in the dark a faint sound of oars came nearer. A clear little bell was tinkling.

"Mother!" somebody was shouting. "Father! I'm coming home!"

"Indeed," said the Hemulen. "My own prisoners! Catch them at once before they burn the theatre down!"

Moominmamma rushed up to the footlights. She saw Moomintroll lose hold of one of his oars when he was about to lay to. Confusedly he tried to pull with the remaining one, but his boat only spun round on the spot. In the stern sat a thin little Hemulen with a kind sort of face and shouting something nobody took any notice of.

"Flee!" cried Moominmamma. "The police are here!"

She didn't know what her Moomintroll had done, but she was convinced that she approved of it.

"Catch the convicts!" now cried the big Hemulen. "They've burned down all the notices in the park and made the Park Keeper luminous!"

The audience had been slightly bewildered for a while, but now they understood that the play was going on. They put away their cups and sat down by the footlights to watch it.

"Catch them!" shouted the fuming Hemulen.

The audience clapped.

"Wait a bit," said Snufkin calmly. "Seems to be a mistake somewhere. Because it was I who tore down those notices. Is the Keeper really luminous still?"

The Hemulen turned and riveted his eyes on him.

"Just fancy what a gain for this Park Keeper," Snufkin continued unconcernedly while he sidled closer and closer to the footlights. "No electricity bills! Perhaps he'll be able to light his pipe on himself and boil eggs on his head."

The Hemulen didn't answer a word. He was coming slowly nearer and opening his huge paws to grasp Snufkin by the collar. Nearer and nearer he came, now he crouched to leap, and the next second . . .

The revolving stage set off at full speed. They could hear Emma laugh, not scornfully this time, but triumphantly.

All at once everything was happening so quickly that the spectators became slightly confused. That was mainly because they all were swept off their feet, pell-mell on the revolving floor. Only the twenty-four little woodies threw themselves at the Hemulen and clung tight on to his tunic.

Snufkin took a flying leap over the footlights and landed in one of the empty boats. Moomintroll's boat tipped over from the surge, and the Snork Maiden, the Fillyjonk, and the Little Hemulen started to swim towards the theatre.

"Bravo! Well done! *Da capo!*"* shouted the audience.

As soon as Moomintroll got his nose over the surface again, he silently turned and swam towards Snufkin's boat. "Hello!" he said and took hold of the gunwale. "I'm awfully glad to see you."

"Hello, hello!" replied Snufkin. "Jump aboard

* Do it again! *Author*.

now, and I'll show you how to make a getaway."

Moomintroll clambered aboard, and Snufkin began pulling seawards with a cascade of foam around the stem.

"Goodbye, all my little children, and thanks for your help!" he cried. "And remember to keep clean and tidy, and don't climb any roofs until the tar is dry!"

The Hemulen in the meantime finally managed to extricate himself from the revolving stage, the woodies, and the cheering spectators who were throwing flowers at him. Violently scolding, he

clambered down in a boat and dashed off in pursuit of Snufkin.

But he was too late; Snufkin had disappeared into the darkness.

Everything became suddenly silent aboard the theatre.

"So you're here now," remarked Emma quietly, fixing her gaze on the drenched Fillyjonk. "But don't imagine that the stage's always a bed of roses."

CHAPTER XIII

About punishment and reward

Snufkin continued to scull in silence for a long time. Moomintroll sat looking at the well-known and comforting outline of his old hat against the night sky and the puffs of pipe-smoke rising in the quiet air. "Everything'll be all right now," he thought.

The shouting and clapping behind them faded slowly away, and after a while the strokes of the oars and the dripping of water were the only sounds to be heard.

The dark streaks of the shores disappeared from sight.

Neither one of the two friends felt any great need of talking. As yet. They had time; summer lay before them, long and full of promises. At this moment their dramatic encounter, the night, and the excitement of the flight were quite enough, something not to be disturbed.

The boat curved back to the near shore again.

Moomintroll realized that Snufkin was leading the pursuers astray. Far away in the darkness shrilled the Hemulen's police whistle, answered by others.

When the boat glided in among the reeds beneath shadowing trees, the full moon was rising from the sea.

"Now listen carefully," said Snufkin.

"Yes," said Moomintroll, and the spirit of adventure sped through his soul on mighty wings.

"You'll have to return to the others at once," said Snufkin. "Then come back to this place with all who want to go back again to Moominvalley. They must leave the furniture at the theatre. And you'll have to hurry away from there before the Hemulens begin keeping guard. I know them. Don't stop on the way, and don't be afraid. The June nights aren't dangerous."

"Yes," said Moomintroll obediently.

He waited a little, but as Snufkin didn't tell him anything more, he climbed ashore and started back along the creek.

Snufkin seated himself in the stern and carefully knocked the ashes from his pipe-bowl. Then he peered out between the reeds. The Hemulen was sculling steadily seawards. He was clearly visible in the moon-path.

Snufkin laughed quietly and began to fill his pipe.

★ ★ ★

The water was going out again at last. Newly washed shores and valleys were slowly creeping up into the sunshine again. The trees were the first to rise over the water. They waved their dazed tops in the air and stretched their branches carefully to feel if they were safe and sound after the disaster. Those that had broken off hurriedly put out new sprouts. The birds found their old sleeping-places again, and higher up on the slopes, where the water had already disappeared, people began spreading out sheets and clothes to dry on the ground.

As soon as the water began falling everybody started for home. People rowed or sailed, night and day, and when the water disappeared they continued afoot to the places where they had lived before.

Possibly some of them had found new and much nicer places during the time the valley was turned into a lake, but still they liked the old places better.

* ★ ★ ★ *

As Moominmamma sat beside her son in the
stern of Snufkin's boat with her handbag in her
lap, she didn't give a thought to the drawing-room
suite she had been compelled to leave behind her.
She thought about her garden, and wondered if
the sea had raked the gravel paths as neatly as she
used to do herself.

Now Moominmamma began to recognize her
surroundings. They were rowing through the pass
to the Lonely Mountains, and she knew that behind

the next turn she would catch sight of the big rock at the entrance to Moominvalley.

"We're coming home, home, home!" Little My was singing in her sister's lap.

The Snork Maiden in the prow was looking down at the underwater-scape. At present there was a meadow beneath the boat, and some of the tallest flowers brushed lightly against the keel. Yellow, red, and blue, they looked up through the clear water and craned their necks towards the sun.

Moominpappa was sculling with long, even strokes.

"Do you think the verandah will be above water?" he asked.

"Time to look when we're there," said Snufkin, looking back over his shoulder.

"Dear me," said Moominpappa. "We've left the Hemulens far behind us."

"Don't be too sure," replied Snufkin.

In the middle of the boat there was a bathing-gown covering a strange little hump. The hump moved. Moomintroll poked lightly at it.

"Won't you come out in the sun for a moment?" he asked.

"No, thanks, I'm really quite all right," a mild voice replied beneath the bathing-gown.

"She gets no air at all, poor little creature," Moominmamma said worriedly. "She's been sitting like that for three whole days."

"Small Hemulens always are shy," Moomintroll

explained in a whisper. "I believe she's crocheting. It makes her feel safer."

But the little Hemulen was not crocheting. She was laboriously writing in an exercise book in black waxcloth covers. "Strictly forbidden," she wrote. "Strictly forbidden, strictly forbidden, strictly forbidden." Five thousand times. It made her comforted and content to fill one page after another.

"How nice it feels to be good," she thought quietly.

Moominmamma squeezed Moomintroll's paw. "What are you thinking about?" she asked.

"I'm thinking of Snufkin's children," replied Moomintroll. "Are they really going to be actors, all of them?"

"Some of them," said his mother. "The Fillyjonk will adopt the untalented ones. She can't manage without relatives."

"They'll miss Snufkin," said Moomintroll sadly.

"Perhaps at first," said Moominmamma. "But he intends calling on them every year and he'll write them birthday letters. With pictures."

Moomintroll nodded. "That's good," he said. "And Whomper and Misabel . . . Did you notice how happy Misabel looked when she first realized that she could stay on at the theatre!"

Moominmamma laughed. "Yes, Misabel was happy. She'll act in tragedies all her life and have a new face each time. And Whomper's the new stage manager and every bit as happy. Isn't it fun when one's friends get exactly what suits them?"

"Yes," said Moomintroll. "Great fun."

At that moment the boat ran aground and stopped.

"We're stuck in the grass," said Moominpappa, peering over the gunwale. "We'll have to wade."

Everybody climbed out from the boat.

The little Hemulen was hiding something obviously very precious under her dress, but nobody asked what it was.

The water still reached up to their waists, and it wasn't easy to make headway, even if the bottom was nice, soft grass and no stones. Here and there it sloped, lifting flowering tussocks like paradise islands over the surface.

Snufkin walked last. He was still more taciturn than usual. He kept looking over his shoulder and listening.

"I'll eat your old hat if they aren't far behind!" said the Mymble's daughter.

But Snufkin only shook his head.

The pass narrowed. Through the opening between the rock-faces shone a glimpse of the friendly greenness of Moominvalley. And a pointed roof with a gaily fluttering flag . . .

Now they could see a turn of the river, with the blue-painted bridge. The jasmines were already in bloom! The Moomins splashed happily onward through the water, talking all at once about everything they were going to do when they came home.

Suddenly a shrill whistle cut the air like a knife.

In a moment the pass was teeming with Hemulens, in front, behind, everywhere.

The Snork Maiden hid her head against Moo-

mintroll's shoulder. No one spoke a word. It was so awful to be nearly home again and caught by the Hemulic police.

The Hemulen came wading towards them. He stopped before Snufkin.

"We-ell?" he said.

Nobody answered.

"We-ell?" said the Hemulen again.

Then the little Hemulen waded up to her cousin as fast as her legs could carry her, dropped a curtsy, and handed him a black exercise book. "Snufkin repents and says he's sorry," she said shyly.

"I've never . . ." Snufkin started to say.

The big Hemulen silenced him with a glance and opened the exercise book. He started to count. He counted a long time. While he was busy the water continued falling and after a while it was only ankle-deep.

Finally the Hemulen said: "Yes, this is quite right. 'Strictly forbidden,' five thousand times."

"But," said Snufkin.

"Please don't say anything," said the little Hemulen. "I've really enjoyed it, honestly I have!"

"What about the notices?" said her cousin.

"Couldn't he put up some new ones instead, around my vegetable plot?" asked Moominmamma. "For instance, 'Visitors are asked to leave a little of the lettuce'?"

"Oh, yes . . . I suppose that would do," replied the Hemulen, slightly crestfallen. "Well, looks like

I'd have to let you off. But don't ever do that again!"

"No," they all said obediently.

"And you're coming home, I think," continued the Hemulen with a severe glance at his little cousin.

"Yes, if you aren't angry with me," she replied. Then she turned to the Moomins and said: "Thanks ever so much for your suggestions about the crocheting. I'll send the slippers as soon as they're finished. What's the address?"

"Moominvalley's enough," said Moominpappa.

★   ★   ★

They ran the last bit. Up the slope, in among the lilac bushes, straight to the front steps. There the Moomins stopped, drawing a long breath of relief and feeling what it felt like to be at home. Everything felt right.

The beautiful fretwork railing on the verandah was unbroken. The sunflower was there. The water barrel was there. And the flood wave had bleached the hammock to a really nice colour. Of the whole flood only a small puddle was left near the front steps, a very suitable swimming-pool for Little My.

It was as if nothing had ever happened and as if no danger could ever threaten them again.

But the gravel paths were strewn with sea shells, and on the porch hung a wreath of red seaweed.

Moominmamma looked up towards the drawing-room window.

"Darling, don't go inside yet," said Moominpappa. "And if you do, keep your eyes shut. I'm going to make a new drawing-room suite as much like the former one as possible. With tassels and red plush and everything."

"There's no need for me to shut my eyes," Moominmamma replied gaily. "I believe the only thing I'm going to miss is a good revolving stage. I think it would be nicer to have mottled plush this time!"

★   ★   ★

In the evening Moomintroll went down to Snufkin's camping place to wish him good night.

Snufkin was having a quiet smoke by the river.

"Everything all right?" asked Moomintroll.

Snufkin nodded. "Absolutely everything," he said.

Moomintroll sniffed. "Have you changed to a new brand?" he asked. "Reminds me of raspberry leaves. Is it good?"

"No," replied Snufkin. "But I smoke it only on Sundays."

"Oh, yes," said Moomintroll a little wonderingly. "It's Sunday, really. Well, cheerio, then, I'm going to bed!"

"Yip, yip!" replied Snufkin.

*   *   *

Moomintroll returned by way of the brown pool behind the hammock tree. He looked down into the water. Yes, the bangles were there.

He began to search the long grass.

It was quite a long time before he found the bark schooner. The back stay had got entangled in a bush, but it was undamaged. Even the little hatch was in its place over the hold.

Moomintroll walked back through the garden to the house. The evening air was cool and mild, and the dewy flowers had a richer fragrance than ever before.

His mother was sitting on the steps. She was waiting for him.

She was holding something in her paws and smiling.

"Know what I've got?" she asked.

"The dinghy!" said Moomintroll, and burst out laughing. Not because anything was especially funny, but just because he felt so very happy.

I am Moominmamma. Turn over and see what Moominpappa has to show you . . .

MOOMIN-GALLERY

I am Moominpappa, but of course, you all know me by now. Here I am in a pensive mood—I wish I knew where that hat disappeared to.

This is Sniff, one of Moomintroll's young friends. A little clumsy sometimes, but means well. After all, the Muddler was his father.

A solitary chap, young Snufkin. Quite unlike the Joxter, his father, but with the same independent outlook on life.

I don't quite know what the Groke is doing here. She isn't much use for anything except as an exclamation!

Ha! here is the would-be-philosopher, our old friend the Muskrat, who likes to be left in peace to think—at least that is what he wants us to believe he is doing.

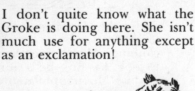

These two are apt to turn up anywhere. Thingumy and Bob —mischievous pair, too fond of pea-shooters and such; but I was young once.

The feminine touch. The Snork Maiden has taken a fancy to Moomintroll, but look what he did for her. Now, I remember when I was a boy . . .

But to proceed. Moomintroll— now there is a chip off the old Moomin block if you like. An eternal reminder of my youth . . .

As for the Hemulen—why do they wear so much clothing? Must remember to look that up—he is our leading Moominphilatelist and also sound on Moominchology.

So, if you want to read more about these curious but likeable inhabitants of Moominland, you should look at the books. I wrote the notes above in 1952, how time goes, and have now added a few more overleaf.

Misabel we met that curious summer. How she enjoyed acting in my plays, and changing clothes.

A tremendous big fellow that Hemulen who invaded the valley one winter. One of those terrific do-gooders. Hmm—bit noisy.

Ah, Too-ticky—much addicted to bathing-houses, the seaside in every particular, in fact, and quite a philosopher in a way.

No selection would be complete without Little My. What would we do without her imperturbability—good word, what! good girl, goodbye for now.